A Frank Marshal Crime Thriller #2

SIMON MCCLEAVE

FALSE WITNESS

by Simon McCleave

A Marshal of Snowdonia Murder Mystery

Frank Marshal Crime Thriller
Book 2

No part of this publication may be reproduced, stored, or transmitted in any form or by any means, electronic, mechanical, photocopying, recording, scanning, or otherwise without written permission from the publisher. It is illegal to copy this book, post it to a website, or distribute it by any other means without permission.

Names, characters, businesses, places, events, and incidents are either the products of the author's imagination or used in a purely fictitious manner. Any resemblance to actual persons, living or dead, or actual events is purely coincidental.

First published by Stamford Publishing Ltd in 2025

Copyright © Simon McCleave, 2025
All rights reserved

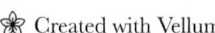 Created with Vellum

BOOKS BY SIMON McCLEAVE

THE DI RUTH HUNTER SERIES

#1. The Snowdonia Killings
#2. The Harlech Beach Killings
#3. The Dee Valley Killings
#4. The Devil's Cliff Killings
#5. The Berwyn River Killings
#6. The White Forest Killings
#7. The Solace Farm Killings
#8. The Menai Bridge Killings
#9. The Conway Harbour Killings
#10. The River Seine Killings
#11. The Lake Vyrnwy Killings
#12. The Chirk Castle Killings
#13. The Portmeirion Killings
#14. The Llandudno Pier Killings
#15. The Denbigh Asylum Killings
#16. The Wrexham Killings
#17. The Colwyn Bay Killings
#18. The Chester Killings
#19. The Llangollen Killings
#20. The Wirral Killings
#21. The Abersoch Killings

THE DC RUTH HUNTER MURDER CASE SERIES

#1. Diary of a War Crime
#2. The Razor Gang Murder
#3. An Imitation of Darkness
#4. This is London, SE15

THE ANGLESEY SERIES - DI LAURA HART

#1. The Dark Tide
#2. In Too Deep
#3. Blood on the Shore
#4. The Drowning Isle
#5. Dead in the Water

PSYCHOLOGICAL THRILLERS

Last Night at Villa Lucia
Five Days in Provence

About the Author

Simon McCleave is a multi million-selling crime novelist who lives in North Wales with his wife and two children.

Before he was an author, Simon worked as a script editor at the BBC and a producer at Channel 4 before working as a story analyst in Los Angeles. He then became a script writer, writing on series such as *Silent Witness*, *The Bill*, *EastEnders* and many more. His Channel 4 film *Out of the Game* was critically acclaimed and described as '*an unflinching portrayal of male friendship*' by *Time Out*.

His first book, *'The Snowdonia Killings'*, was released in January 2020 and soon became an Amazon Bestseller, reaching No 1 in the UK Chart and selling over 400,000 copies. His twenty subsequent novels in the DI Ruth Hunter Snowdonia Series have all been Amazon bestsellers, with most of them hitting the top of the digital charts. He has sold over 3 million books to date.

'The Dark Tide', Simon's first book in an Anglesey based crime series for publishing giant Harper Collins (Avon), was a major hit in 2022, becoming the highest selling Waterstone's Welsh Book of the Month ever.

This year, Simon is releasing the first in a new series of books, *'Marshal of Snowdonia'* with several more planned for 2025.

Simon has also written a one-off psychological thriller, *Last Night at Villa Lucia*, for Storm Publishing, which was a major hit, *The Times* describing it as '*...well above the usual seasonal villa thriller...*' with its '*...empathetic portrayal of lives spent in the shadow of coercion and abuse.*'

The Snowdonia based DI Ruth Hunter books are now set to be filmed as a major new television series, with shooting to begin in North Wales in 2025.

Your FREE book is waiting for you now!

Get your FREE copy of the prequel to
the DI Ruth Hunter Series NOW
http://www.simonmccleave.com/vip-email-club
and join my VIP Email Club

Prologue

Sunday 1st January, 2023

MARCUS HAD POPPED out of the back of his cottage for a quick smoke. He peered intently into the darkness. The back garden, large gravel driveway and old brick feed shed were veiled in fog. It was so thick that only the outlines rather than colours or details were visible. There was a deathly silence. That's why Marcus loved it here. Peace and quiet. Apart from the handful of cottages, they were in the middle of nowhere. Bliss.

As he took a long, deep drag on his cigar, a red firework exploded high up in the sky. Then it fell slowly with showers of silver. And although it was beautiful, the noise had jarred on Marcus' nerves. Having served in the army for a decade and fought in Desert Storm, Marcus had dealt with both mental health and other issues, but he'd never been diagnosed with PTSD. However, decades later, any sudden noise like a firework still instantly put his nervous system on red alert.

Taking another long drag on his cigar, Marcus blew the smoke up into the air, trying to calm himself. His heart was thumping in his chest. Maybe he should finish his cigar quickly and go back inside.

Glancing up at the enormous dark sky that was scattered with silver stars, Marcus managed to get some perspective. It was New Year's Eve. He'd had a few drinks with his wife Sian and an old friend, Ollie, in the afternoon. Then a quiet meal with his wife. They'd even cuddled on the sofa in front of the television. It'd been a while since they'd done that. He was glad they'd managed to resolve some of their differences. The past three to four months had taken their toll on their marriage. It was his fault. It was always his fault. He knew that he was to blame in his slightly drunken state in the pitch dark. It's just that he never wanted to admit it. Marcus was a proud man. He found it difficult to admit that he was ever wrong.

Tilting up his head, he saw that the soft edges of the vanilla moon had now hardened like the rind on a good cheese. He and Sian owned their cottage. It was situated close to Llanelltyd, a small village in Gwynedd, just northwest of Dolgellau in the heart of Eryri National Park. Or Snowdonia, as the English liked to call it. Just after lunch, he, Sian and Ollie had all hiked up to Cymer Abbey, which was about three miles away. Built in the 12th century, the ruins of the abbey were in a picturesque setting beside the River Mawddach. It was one of Marcus' favourite walks. The ruins had once been a Cistercian monastery originally founded under the patronage of two brothers, Gruffudd and Maredudd, grandsons of King Owain Gwynedd. The abbey was said to have been cursed by the monks when they were expelled during Henry VIII's dissolution of the monasteries in the 1500s. Visitors claimed to have seen the hooded ghosts of monks wandering the ruins especially at first daylight. Marcus was still waiting for his ghostly encounter as he was often up there with Beamish, his chocolate Labrador, at dawn.

Marcus just loved the mythology and history of the place, and even though none of them had spotted any ghostly monks that afternoon, Beamish had acted very strangely. He'd barked and whined, clearly upset and disturbed by something within the ruins. Ollie made a big joke out of it, but Marcus knew that Beamish had sensed something there.

Dragging hard again on his cigar, Marcus blew a long plume of smoke up into the night sky. He watched as the wind grabbed the white smoke and flung it away with a dramatic twist, like a vanishing ghost. He then caught the scent of the surrounding countryside. Damp grass, heather, and the redolent odour of the log fire they had lit inside the cottage. It reminded him of his childhood days, playing outside on the family farm close to Corris, a small village about ten miles south from where they were. His father Richard, a school teacher, had put a lot of pressure on him and his sister, Glynis, to do well academically. He wanted them to do A-levels and go to college or university. Marcus had a deep distrust and dislike of his father. He'd heard people referring to him as 'a ladies' man'. As far as Marcus could see, his father had had a string of affairs which his mother chose to ignore. So, he could stick A-levels and university up his arse. Marcus couldn't wait to get away, which is why he left to join the Welsh Guards in 1988. The regiment had then been posted to the Gulf and fought in Desert Storm in 1991. That's where he'd met his friend Ollie who had been over that afternoon. There was nothing like active combat to create lifelong friendships between men. They'd been through something together that no one else could understand.

Since leaving the Welsh Guards, the members of his platoon had all gone on to different careers, with varying success. And they had all developed Gulf War Syndrome, a chronic illness that affected over 30,000 British soldiers who fought in that conflict. Research suggested that the syndrome had been caused by exposure to the nerve agent Sarin, which had been released into the air when the Iraqi chemical weapon depots and stores were bombed by the allies. Marcus didn't know much more than that. What he did know is that it had blighted all their lives over the years.

Then he heard the faintest of noises which broke his train of thought. It sounded like a car engine. Turning to look at the road, he saw the headlights of a car approaching. It was almost 1am. Probably someone heading home after a New Year's Eve party. He wondered if they were over the drink/drive limit and risking it on the deserted roads of Eryri. Dozens did, especially at this time of year. Marcus couldn't remember the last time he'd seen a marked police car driving down this road. It was months ago. He'd read about the budgets for North Wales Police being cut in the paper a few weeks ago.

He squinted at the headlights. The vehicle was a large black 4x4. Something flash and expensive. Maybe a Range Rover Sport or a BMW X4. It was hard to tell, as the road was shrouded in thick fog giving the whole scene a slightly sinister feel. The car slowed down to a stop. It then waited for about ten seconds, drove slowly for about twenty yards, before pulling away at high speed, its tyres screeching slightly on the road surface.

That's very weird, Marcus thought to himself. *Could be a lost tourist, I suppose.*

Eryri/Snowdonia National Park was full of tourists at this time of the year. And most of them were bloody English!

He flicked his cigar butt away, watching its orange glow disappear into the long, damp grass. Then he heard the sound of footsteps on the gravel pathway that came down the side of the cottage to the small patio at the back.

Who's that?

It had to be Sian. There was no one else at the cottage.

'Alright, alright, love,' he laughed. 'I'm coming.'

The footsteps stopped.

Silence.

Suddenly a crow cawed overhead, making him jump.

Jesus! Where the hell has Sian gone?

'Hello?' Marcus called out, looking around and feeling a little on edge.

Nothing.

Suddenly, he saw a figure in a hood approaching. They held a powerful torch in their hand that completely dazzled him.

Marcus put his hand up to shield his eyes from the glare. 'I just said I'm coming back, Sian,' he said in frustration.

He felt someone grab his arms from behind and put him in a restraining hold. He tried to resist but they were strong.

He spun to see who was behind him but it was too dark.

'Oi, what's going on?' he shouted.

Everything was happening so fast.

Chapter 1

I stirred in my sleep and heard voices talking in my head. It was the history podcast that I'd been listening to when I'd fallen asleep. The true story of the outlaw *Jessie James*. Much to my disappointment, the myth that *Jessie James* had been some sort of Robin Hood character, robbing trains and stagecoaches in the Old West and giving the money to the poor, was a fabrication.

The tiny bud headphones were still in my ears. In the darkness, I glanced at my phone. It was 4.23am. The dead of night. But something was wrong. Our trusty German Shepherd, Jack, had stirred at the foot of our bed and was now sitting up straight. Even in the darkness I could see that his ears were pointed up and alert. He'd heard something.

Pulling the earbuds from my ears, I leaped out of bed.

'What is it, boy?' I whispered to him.

Pulling the curtains back, I looked outside. It was dark. Nothing had tripped the light sensors, but Jack jumped up at the windowsill and then growled and whined. Whatever he'd sensed, it had clearly disturbed him. And I trusted Jack's instincts more than the light sensors outside.

Something was wrong.

I grabbed my dressing gown and padded quickly across the bedroom, leaving my wife Rachel to sleep peacefully.

It had only been three months since my daughter's partner, TJ, a feckless minor drug dealer, had turned up here brandishing a knife in the middle of the night. He'd banged loudly on the front door of the annexe of our farmhouse, demanding to see my grandson, Sam. My daughter, Caitlin, had left TJ and their home in North London only a few days earlier after he'd hit her. It was my assumption that it wasn't the first time he'd been physically abusive towards her by any stretch of the imagination. Brandishing my shotgun, I'd eventually managed to overpower him and get the knife from him until the police arrived.

Jack and I now jogged down the stairs and headed along the hallway to the front door. Opening it, I peered out cautiously. A blast of cold air hit my face.

I listened intently as I stared into the blackness of the night.

Nothing.

Just the deep groan of the wind that rolled in across the fields from the mountains of Eryri. The rustling of the last few leaves on a nearby tree.

As a former detective in the North Wales Police force – thirty-five years – I'd hoped that TJ would be charged with aggravated burglary, which carried a maximum sentence of life imprisonment. However, he'd actually been charged with a lesser offence, along with possession of Class A drugs. Caitlin and I had been baffled and very disappointed. TJ had been released on bail with a curfew, but now we had no idea where he was. He'd made it clear to officers on his release that he had no intention of returning to London. And his exact words to Detective Sergeant Kelly Thomas were *I'm not going anywhere without my son*. I'd been livid. It wasn't Kelly's fault. The charges were decided by the lawyers at the Crown Prosecution Service.

Since the news of TJ's bail, we'd been living in a heightened sense of anxiety in case he returned. I'd beefed up the security in the past twelve weeks. There were now lights with sensors along the driveway up to our farmhouse. I'd fitted a video doorbell and cameras to both the annexe where Caitlin and Sam now lived, and our front door. Plus, I'd reinforced all the doors at both properties.

Finally, I'd bought in a fresh supply of shotgun cartridges for my Winchester Select shotgun. If that little fucker turned up here again, I was more than prepared to blow his head off with no remorse. I thought about Sam, Caitlin, and Rachel, and knew all our lives would be significantly safer and better if TJ was no longer on the planet. And that suited me fine. After all, I was an expert on the self-defence and reasonable force laws of the land. If I decided to shoot TJ, there would be no way that I'd be serving any time.

My eyes scanned the whole area outside again. I wasn't satisfied that nobody was out there. Not when it came to my daughter and grandson. Moving swiftly back to the living room, I unlocked my steel gun case. Inside was my pride and joy. My Winchester Select shotgun. A dark mahogany stock, with silver casing, barrels and an adjustable trigger. It was a beauty, with the classic American over/under barrels, rather than the more traditional British side by side. Definitely more accurate over long range.

I caught a waft of gun oil as I grabbed the gun, then

turned and headed outside with Jack, popping cartridges into the Winchester and loading as I went.

Bounding away, Jack's movement immediately set off the motion-sensored lights. The whole area was illuminated.

Right, let's see if there's anyone out here, I thought to myself as I nestled the stock of the shotgun into the nook of my shoulder. Raising the gun up to my eyeline, I put my finger on the cold steel trigger and moved forward cautiously.

Jack circled back, sniffing at the grass and the air, trying to lock on to a scent.

'What is it, Jack?' I asked him with a sense of urgency.

If there had been someone out there who he didn't know, he would have started to bark immediately. And probably given them a decent bite too.

He sat by my feet for a few seconds as I scanned the area again.

The vanilla-coloured moon sat low, and the ink-black sky was scattered with silver stars that glowed and sparkled. If it wasn't for the current situation, it'd be a perfect winter's night.

And it was now 2023. Just.

Happy New Year, Frank, I said to myself, wondering how on earth it could be 2023. It blew my mind. I'd been born in 1953, the year of Queen Elizabeth II's coronation. Winston Churchill had been the Prime Minister.

Dear God. Where has all that time gone?

The lights went out as Jack was sitting still beside me. I reached down and put my hand on his head to reassure him. 'It's all right, boy,' I said quietly.

The wind picked up and a leaf skittered noisily along the bumpy driveway before diving into a pothole full of muddy water.

Then everything went still.

Maybe Jack had been spooked by a rabbit or a hare? Or even a fox. Whatever it was, it had gone.

FLASH!

The lights burst into life again.

They startled me and I jumped.

Jesus! What the hell set them off?

I gripped the gun tightly.

Now with a furrowed forehead, I scoured the whole area for a clue as to what was setting off the motion sensors.

Then out of the corner of my eye, I saw movement over by the annexe where Caitlin and Sam were tucked up in bed.

I tapped at my thigh and looked at Jack. 'Stay close to me, boy,' I whispered.

I peered again.

A figure was standing outside the annexe, tucked behind one of the solid wooden pillars that held up the old porch.

You fucker, I thought, as my nostrils flared and I gritted my teeth.

How dare that prick come back here.

My heart started to pound against my chest as I took a deep breath to steady myself. Getting angry was only going to make me irrational and jumpy.

With the thumb of my right hand, I clicked off the Winchester's safety catch.

I took a step forward towards the annexe.

Jack made a little whine and I reassured him. 'It's okay, boy.' He could sense my anxiety but was well trained enough to stick by my side.

As I took a few more steps forward, I wondered why Jack hadn't sensed TJ hiding up by the annexe. It seemed strange. Maybe he was losing his touch. Or maybe the strong winds had just made it difficult to get a scent.

I could just make out the shape of someone's head and shoulders.

Taking a few more steps, I got to the little paved path that led down to the front door.

I got a whiff of something strange on the air. Something sweet and sickly.

TJ wasn't moving. Had he spotted me and was now hiding?

Was he armed? The last time he'd arrived wielding a large kitchen knife.

I reassured myself that I had the Winchester and Jack for protection.

As I took another step, I trod on a rogue twig which snapped loudly.

I froze.

The figure moved from behind the wooden pillar.

'STAY WHERE YOU ARE!' I bellowed at the top of my voice as my pulse raced.

Jack barked, but not as ferociously as I would have expected him to.

My eyes adjusted.

If he's armed and takes one step towards you, shoot him, I told myself.

My mouth was dry.

The figure was wearing a big black padded coat and a black ski hat pulled down low over their forehead.

My finger quivered on the trigger.

This is it.

If he made a dash towards me, I was prepared to shoot him dead.

'Dad?' said a voice.

Caitlin?

The figure standing in front of me was my daughter.

'Jesus fucking Christ, Caitlin, I nearly bloody shot you!' I thundered angrily.

'Oh God, sorry,' she said, pulling an apologetic face.

'Sorry?' I snapped, letting out a frustrated sigh of relief.

I put the safety catch on and lowered the gun.

Jack trotted over to her and she squatted down to pat and scruff his head. That explained Jack's lack of reaction to someone being out here.

'What the bloody hell are you doing?' I demanded angrily. I'd nearly killed her.

She gave me an apologetic shrug. 'Sorry. I'm really sorry, Dad.'

Then I saw the green plastic tube in her hand. A vape.

'You were out here bloody vaping?' I asked, shaking my head.

She nodded. 'Yeah, I don't like doing it indoors. And I don't want Sam to see me.'

'Not worth getting bloody killed for though is it?'

'Not really.'

'Jesus, Caitlin!' I gave her a withering look. 'I've spent the last three months trying to make this place safer than the ruddy White House. And you've just decided to stand outside at four o'clock in the morning having a vape, or whatever it is you're doing.' I was aware that my anger and frustration were giving me a tight chest.

'I've said I'm sorry, Dad,' she replied, 'but you need to calm down or you'll give yourself a heart attack at your age.'

I let out a growl. Telling me to calm down and then reminding me that I was an old man wasn't the best way to get me to relax.

'What were you thinking?' I asked in an icy tone.

She tried to reassure me. 'I'll be alright. After all, I

think I'd notice a car coming up here at four in the morning.'

I looked at her with narrowed eyes, then pointed angrily to the dark fields around us. 'Ever thought that TJ might park away from here and then come to the annexe on foot? I know he's a complete moron but I doubt even he's stupid enough to just drive up here.'

Caitlin pulled another apologetic face. 'Fair point. I'm an idiot.'

'You are an idiot.' I allowed myself a half smile, then sighed, taking a long deep breath. 'And I didn't even know you vaped.'

'Well, I do,' she conceded. 'I just don't do it while you're around because you'll give me a disapproving look and tell me I'm wasting money.'

'Which you are,' I snapped. 'You didn't used to smoke, did you?'

The expression on her face told me the answer.

'For God's sake, Caitlin,' I groaned.

'Hypocrite,' she replied, with an amused lift of her eyebrow.

'I haven't smoked for bloody years,' I protested. 'Nearly thirty years to be precise. Not since your Taid died from lung cancer in 1993. I stamped on my cigarettes outside the hospital, put them in the bin, and that was that.'

Caitlin sighed. 'I don't smoke.'

'What the hell is that anyway?'

'Kiwi and watermelon. Want to try some?'

'Erm, definitely not,' I said, but my face finally broke into a half smile as my heart rate returned to normal. Then I held out my hand. 'Go on then.'

She pulled a face. 'Really?'

'Give it here.' I took the vape from her and put it to my lips. I sucked, and my mouth filled with sweet, disgusting vapour. I coughed and grimaced. 'Bloody hell, that's disgusting. How do you smoke that crap?'

'Not a fan then, Dad?' she asked sardonically.

'Make sure you don't let Sam see you doing that,' I said. 'I don't want him getting any stupid ideas.'

There were a few seconds of silence as my breathing and pulse finally returned to normal. I took a long deep breath of cold air.

'Is Mum okay?' Caitlin asked.

'Yeah, she's fine. Fast asleep.'

We'd all stayed up in the living room to see in the New Year. My wife, Rachel, suffers from Lewes body dementia. It comes and goes, but it's heartbreaking to see her lost for words or memories. Caitlin had put on some old Elvis and Dean Martin songs and Rachel perked up and sang her heart out. She particularly liked *Return to Sender*. I wondered how many more New Years I'd get to see in with her but I tried not to think about it.

'Right, I'm going back inside,' I said, pointing back to the main farmhouse. 'Early start.'

Caitlin nodded with a smile. 'Sam's very excited. He's really taken to riding thanks to you.'

I laughed. 'Hey, he's a natural. Chip off the old block, eh?'

'Night Dad,' she said with a grin. 'Love you.'

'I love you too, darling.' I turned and felt Jack come to my side as we walked back to the house. 'And stop vaping will you?'

Chapter 2

I pulled the reins on my horse Duke to slow him to a stop. 'Woah, there.' He gave a deep neigh as steam plumed out of his nostrils into the icy air. Duke was my chestnut-coloured cob and checked in at a mighty seventeen hands. He was probably too big for a man of seventy, but I didn't care if it took me longer to get my foot up into the stirrup.

It was early on New Year's Day. The landscape around us was white and brittle with frost. A sharp breeze swished away the clouds made by my breath. Down to my right, Jack had stopped, his tongue hanging and his breath laboured from keeping up. But his tail wagged. He was enjoying this cross-country trek.

Turning back, I saw that my ten-year-old grandson Sam was just behind on his beautiful white Connemara pony called Lleuad, which was Welsh for moon. I'd bought Lleuad for him three months ago.

'Taid,' he called over with a grimace, 'my butt hurts.'

'Your butt?' I laughed. I'd spent the past three months teaching him to ride and he was starting to get the hang of it. 'Remember what I told you. You've got to post the trot to feel the timing of his hooves. If you get stuck, stand up for a moment. And keep counting.'

Sam nodded but looked disheartened.

'Hey, mate,' I said reassuringly. 'Think about what your riding was like when you first got him. You've done a grand job. I'm really proud of you.'

A little smile flickered on Sam's ruddy face. That's all I needed to see to know I was on the right track.

'You tired?' I asked.

He nodded.

'Hungry?'

He nodded again.

We'd been going across country for about an hour. I pointed over to the south. 'We'll loop back that way via the old abbey and go home, okay? Last one back makes the hot chocolate.'

Sam smiled. 'Deal.'

'Come on, boy,' I said to Duke as I dug my heels into his side and we moved off. His hooves crunched on the frost-hardened ground beneath us like the sound of crisps.

As we went, I looked over at the vast rugged landscape. Over to our left, beyond the dry stone wall that snaked away into the distance, the frost-dusted land was scarred by rivulet marks where ploughs had crossed and recrossed. In the distance, the mighty Cadair Idris mountain, which was plum-coloured in the early morning light, loomed over us as if watching our progress. Its peak was sprinkled with snow. The mountain lay at the southern end of Eryri National Park and translated from Welsh as *Idris' Chair*. I preferred the folktale that Idris had not only been a giant, but also a philosopher, astronomer, and poet. He'd used the mountain as a chair from which he could contemplate the stars and the meaning of the universe. Legend had it that if you slept a whole night on the top of Cadair Idris, you would go mad and commit murderous acts against those you loved. It wasn't something I was going to put to the test.

The wind picked up and cut at my face, numbing the tip of my nose and the tops of my ears. The sky above us was starting to darken with rain clouds which soon covered the early morning sun like sluggish columns of smoke.

This time alone out in the wilderness with Sam gave me time to contemplate the past three months, which had been challenging for all of us to say the least. I was glad that it was now a new year and we could use it as a restart.

Reaching the Afon Mawddach, a river that ran north to south through the national park, we started to follow it north with the ruins of Cymer Abbey over to our left. There were a few old cottages to our right that I knew had been renovated in recent years. Some were now rented out through Airbnb. One of them had decking and a hot tub. I thought about trying to explain to my own Taid that wealthy people would sit in a pool of hot bubbling water in the middle of winter and think it was the height of luxury. He would think that was crazy. Which of course it was.

I'd never been on the Airbnb website, but all I knew is that I'd seen a lot more Range Rovers, green Hunter wellies, and black labradors in the area than ever before. And no one who arrived looked or sounded Welsh.

The cottage closest to us had smoke coming from a chimney. The edges of the roof and guttering were crusted with thick ice. Like most of the cottages here, it dated back to the 19th century and was made from uncoursed rubble stone – essentially broken up boulders. Originally it would have been whitewashed using crushed and heated limestone, which was far cheaper than paint. Of course, they had all now been newly whitewashed with Farrow and Ball masonry paint. I thought Farrow and

Ball were a comedy duo from the 1970s, but what do I know?

Out of the corner of my eye, I noticed a woman in her early 50s running down a track and away from what looked like an old, disused stone farm building.

Her face was ashen and her eyes wide with panic. Something about her expression and the way she ran made me stop in my tracks. She looked distraught.

'Everything all right?' I called over, instinctively knowing that something was actually very wrong.

She looked over at me, searching for words. 'No.' She shook her head as her eyes filled with tears. 'It's my husband …' She gestured back to the building with a horrified expression. 'He …' She couldn't seem to find the words to finish her sentence.

I'd already started to dismount. 'Is your husband all right?' I asked.

'No. No, he's not,' the woman whispered, lost in her thoughts. There was a discernible darkness to the way she said it.

'Anything I can do to help?' I asked, although I was now fearing the worst.

I glanced over at Sam who looked confused. 'Stay there, mate. I'm just going to have a look and see if I can help.'

Sam nodded, not quite sure what was going on.

I gave a little whistle and Jack immediately came to my side.

The woman pointed towards the cottage. 'I need to get a knife. I can't leave him like that. And I need to ring the police.'

'Okay,' I said immediately, going into detective mode. The fact that she wanted to get a knife and didn't want to *leave him like that* made me wonder if her husband had taken himself to that building and hanged himself. I didn't know what else she could have meant by that.

I tied Duke to the wooden fence and jogged across the gravelled driveway towards the stone building where I'd seen the woman coming from. Jack trotted alongside me. The single-storey building didn't look like it was part of the grounds of the house. It was about twenty yards from the farmhouse. It had small square unglazed openings to let in light. The double doors at its rear had been boarded up with wooden slats. The roof was made of dark slate and was in need of repair.

At first, I couldn't see a way to get inside. Then I turned down the flank of the building and saw a door-sized space in the stonework. The exterior walls were covered in a white frosty cloak of dark green moss and lichen. The air smelled damp.

Not knowing what I was going to be faced with, I approached the doorway slowly and then looked inside.

Jack glanced up at me cautiously. He could sense my apprehension.

'It's okay, boy,' I reassured him. 'Stay with me.'

The interior was dark with a dirty stone floor.

And hanging from the central beam of wood was a man who was in his 50s.

Oh God.

My suspicions were correct.

The scene hit me like a steam train. In some ways, it shouldn't have done. I'd seen my fair share of suicides as a police officer.

My mouth went dry as I swallowed. My breathing became shallow.

I was instantly transported back to ten years ago.

May 2012. A date that was etched into the darkness of my very soul.

My son, James, had come back from London to live with us. His mental health issues had got progressively worse through his 20s. And then on the 21st May he disappeared from our farmhouse. I knew that he hadn't gone far as his car was still outside. I'd searched the local woods at the back of where we lived and found him hanging from the branch of a tree. Having managed to cut his body down, I carried him back to our farmhouse. When Rachel had seen me approaching, she'd let out a piercing wail like a wounded animal. I'd never experienced emotional pain like it. I knew I never would again. And I knew that I'd never get over it.

Seeing the man hanging there brought all those feelings back. I took a sharp intake of breath to steady myself. My pulse was racing.

Sensing that something was wrong, Jack gave a little whine as he kept close to my side. I reached down and put my hand on his head. 'It's all right, Jack,' I whispered.

I walked slowly over to where the man was hanging. Even though it was hard to tell in the light, he seemed to have dark olive skin. Maybe Mediterranean or even Arabic. For a moment, I thought I recognised him from somewhere. It was hard to tell. His face was bloated.

To one side, there was a small aluminium stepladder. He'd clearly used this to climb up, attach the rope, and then step off. But something wasn't quite right. The position of the stepladder was off.

I peered at it. At the top of the steps were two arched handles. The man would have needed to stand on the top step, given the height of the makeshift noose he'd created. But if he'd stepped off the top of those steps directly right, as his position showed he had, his legs would have knocked the handle and the stepladder would have either moved or fallen over. It had done neither. Instead, it was perfectly positioned. It was too perfect.

That doesn't add up, I thought as I started to become suspicious.

Taking out my phone, I turned on its torch and went nearer to the stepladder to inspect it. There were clumps of thick mud on the top two steps.

I reached into my pocket and pulled out a biro. Moving closer, I pushed the tip of the pen into the mud. It was still damp. Given that we'd had rain overnight, the mud was fresh. This didn't prove anything until I'd checked the man's footwear.

I used the torch to inspect his shoes and saw that he was wearing slippers. With the exception of a couple of small stones and a few flakes of dark earth, the soles were relatively clean. They certainly didn't match the mud that was on the steps. There was only one conclusion. The man hanging in this building didn't use the stepladder – someone else did. And if the man didn't climb up the stepladder and step off to hang himself, how the hell did he manage to get himself up there?

There was something incredibly suspicious about the whole scene.

Someone else had been here.

THE WOMAN CAME BACK, her eyes wild with anguish. She was holding a large kitchen knife.

'I've called the police,' she gasped. Her whole body was shaking.

She was wearing green leggings and a black sweatshirt. Her bobbed auburn hair had been tied into a stubby ponytail and her face was scraped of all make-up.

'Okay,' I said.

She looked at me. 'Can you help me get him down from there?'

I shook my head. It was a suspicious death. We couldn't touch anything.

'I'm really sorry, but we need to wait for the police to get here,' I explained as gently as I could.

The woman looked distressed and shook her head. 'No. No, I can't just leave him there.'

'The police will be here soon. And I know this is very hard, but you have to leave him,' I said a little more firmly. I understood that her overwhelming instinct was to get him down. That leaving him there like that was cruel, even barbaric – but he was gone.

She looked at me, her face bewildered and in shock.

'I used to be a detective in the North Wales Police,' I reassured her. 'Come on. Let's go back to your house.'

Chapter 3

Annie was lying awake, staring up at the ceiling cornice. A small cobweb looped across like a tiny hammock. She looked at the clock on her bedside table. 8.38am. Even though last night had been New Year's Eve, she'd been tucked up in bed at 10.30pm with a good book. A biography of her heroine, Emmeline Pankhurst, the political activist who led the British suffragette movement and eventually helped women win the right to vote in the UK in 1918. Then Annie had woken at 3.30am with the book lying on her chest. Since then, she hadn't really slept at all.

It was only her second week in her new home, and it was hard to get used to being somewhere new. The little creaks and sounds. The layout of the bedroom and the position of the window. Everything felt different. And in reality, everything <u>was</u> different. A new bed, mostly new furniture, bedding, and towels. She'd burned everything that had been touched by her monster of a husband, Stephen. There was no way that she was going to sleep in the same bed as the one she'd shared with him sporadically. Or use a towel that he'd touched. In a fit of rage, she'd burned his clothes and books, and smashed everything that he'd held dear. The little trinkets, school reports, photographs of Stephen as a child; they'd all gone into a satisfying inferno in their back garden. She wanted to eradicate every trace of him from the planet. When the undertakers had asked her if she'd like a memorial plaque for him at the Bangor Crematorium, she had snorted *Definitely not.*

And there was no way that she could have returned to the house she'd shared with that wicked man for over forty years. Three months ago, Annie's life had been turned upside down. In fact, that didn't really describe the destruction and pain that had shattered her life. It was like some terrible nightmare that, even three months on, she still thought she was going to wake up from.

To her horror, she'd discovered that Stephen had murdered her younger sister, Meg. Annie was beyond heartbroken. She and Meg had been so incredibly close. As if this wasn't enough for her to bear, it had become clear that Stephen was a serial killer who had murdered at least three women in North Wales in the late 1990s. It just made her shudder and her skin crawl. She wasn't even sure it was something that she was ever going to get over. Just trying to get her head around the fact that she had shared her life, her home, and her bed with a man who had murdered innocent women made her physically sick.

Annie had spent the last three months trawling her memory for signs that Stephen was a psychopath and a monster. But there was nothing glaringly obvious. He found intimacy uncomfortable sometimes. She'd put that down to his age, and an education at a strict Catholic boarding school in the days where boys were beaten if they stepped an inch out of line. She'd even wondered if Stephen had been abused while he was there. She remembered the terrible scandal surrounding Ampleforth College, a Catholic boarding school in North Yorkshire. An inquiry had found that monks and lay members of staff had abused and molested boys at the school in the 1970s.

It was the burning question that had often troubled her as a judge, and now plagued her after the sickening truth about her husband. It wasn't the how or the what. It was the why? She needed to try and make sense of what he'd done. Was it some neural abnormality that had robbed Stephen of all empathy and a moral code? Was that just the hand that nature or genetics had dealt him? She tried to remember what his parents had been like. Was the clue somewhere in there? It had to be, didn't it? Annie knew from the hundreds of cases that she'd dealt with, a criminal's background and childhood played such a fundamental and pivotal role in shaping a person's personality, their ability to feel compassion and know right from wrong. But in seeking that, was she also trying to find a way of forgiving or even exonerating Stephen? From what she could recall, his father had been a cold, cruel man who'd sent his two sons away to a Scottish boarding school at the age of six. But there were thousands of other children who'd been through the same without becoming serial killers.

Maybe her quest lay in her own feelings of guilt. That somehow she bore some responsibility for Stephen's murderous nature. After all, how could she not have spotted it? Annie remembered wondering how Sonia Sutcliffe, the wife of the Yorkshire Ripper, could not have known that her husband had been roaming the streets of Leeds and Bradford, brutally murdering thirteen women. How could she not have known, despite what she claimed? Sonia Sutcliffe had been working as a teacher while her husband carried out his reign of terror and claimed to have had no idea. Detectives confirmed that it was their belief she was completely oblivious, based on a phone call Peter Sutcliffe made to her telling her, 'It's me love. I'm the Yorkshire Ripper.'

But now Annie knew that it was possible to be married to a monster and just not realise. Of course, she knew all the research. She'd worked as a Crown Court Judge for over twenty-five years. The dark irony is that she'd sat in judgement over three serial killers in that time. She understood that they felt no compassion or empathy for other human beings. That they were arch manipulators and that they were able to completely compartmentalise their terrible crimes and continue to live a seemingly 'normal' life.

It was such a crushing, devastating thought. It was as if someone had pulled the rug from under Annie's feet so that everything she had thought was true about her life in the past forty years was now gone. It was fake. A lie. A terrible lie.

Blowing out her cheeks, Annie sat up in her bed. It was exhausting trying to process all these thoughts and feelings. Desperately trying to reach some kind of conclusion that might eventually lead to closure. But she refused to cry again so she gritted her teeth.

Come on Annie, up you get!

She knew the only way to survive was to keep busy and not sit and dwell on it. She'd get dressed and have coffee and breakfast for starters. New Year's Day.

Her phone buzzed with a message.

HAPPY NEW YEAR, *Mum. Let's hope 2023 is a much better year. I know you've been through so much recently. Looking forward to seeing you later. Love Meredith xx*

. . .

ANNIE'S HEART warmed at the message. It struck her that it still sometimes felt strange when she read the word *Mum*. Maybe it's because to the outside world, she didn't have any children. Meredith was her secret that she'd kept hidden for half a century.

In 1967, Annie had become pregnant after a drunken one night stand. She was seventeen. Her daughter, Meredith, had been given up for adoption. In 2007, Meredith had made contact with Annie. She was a single mum with a 16-year-old son, Ethan. After a few tense meetings, Annie and Meredith agreed that they wanted to be in each other's lives. However, Annie hadn't told a soul about who Meredith or Ethan were. Not even her best friend, Frank, who had been with her to meet Ethan at their flat in Corwen.

It was a secret that weighed heavily on her. Especially now that Meredith had recently been diagnosed with breast cancer.

Chapter 4

'Here you go, Sian,' I said, as I placed a mug of hot tea in front of her on the long oak table in the farmhouse's kitchen.

'Thank you,' she whispered, looking lost. She hardly registered me as I sat down.

For the past ten minutes, I'd been talking to her. Her husband was called Marcus. He had been 53 years old. At this stage, it wasn't for me to flag up that I was having my doubts that he'd actually taken his own life and that there was something suspicious about what I'd seen.

Ten minutes ago I'd gone outside, helped Sam to dismount and tie up his pony Lleuad to the fence next to Duke. Sam was now sitting in a big wooden rocking chair over by the AGA drinking a mug of hot chocolate. Jack was sitting at his feet having a rest, his big brown eyes surveying the room. I'd called Caitlin, and she was on her way over to pick Sam up. I didn't want him to be around for any longer than he needed to be.

I glanced around the kitchen. It was modern-looking although there was a cream-coloured AGA on the far side.

There was also a Welsh dresser that had various bits of distinctive Portmeirion china on it. Over by the sink were empty bottles of Prosecco, red wine, plus some cans of beer. On the wall next to us was a framed photo of a huddle of soldiers. It looked like it had been taken somewhere in the Middle East. The soldiers were posed in desert camouflage with a background of netting, khaki tents, and sand dunes.

I sipped my tea and pointed to the photo. 'Marcus was in the army?'

Sian nodded. 'Welsh Guards, but he left the army a long time ago.'

I did a quick calculation of his age and the photo. 'Was he in Iraq?'

'No.' She shook her head. 'Gulf War.'

Silence. I didn't want to bombard her with questions about Marcus. She was still in a terrible state of shock.

'He retrained as a geography teacher,' she then said in a virtual whisper.

Her words struck a chord with me.

'Marcus Daniels?' I asked, now realising that I had indeed recognised him. I'd known his parents, Richard and Indira, very well. Indira had died from a series of major strokes about three years ago and Rachel and I had attended the funeral.

I was a bit thrown that I just hadn't recognised Marcus.

Sian took a second to process my question and then looked confused. 'You knew him?'

'Yes. Richard, his father, is an old friend of mine from way back. And my son James went to St Mary's school. Marcus taught him for a couple of years.' In my mind I got the flash of a memory of Rachel, James and I sitting across a small desk from Marcus at a Parents' Evening. Marcus had been so encouraging and positive about

James' work that night. I remembered how proud of James I was.

'Oh right,' Sian said with a nervous blink. 'Richard was a teacher too. Science.'

'Of course,' I said. 'I know that my son James thought the world of Marcus as a teacher.' There was an awkward silence as I sipped my tea and then glanced over at Sam. 'You okay, mate?' I asked.

He nodded but went immediately back to whatever he was watching on his phone.

Even though Sam hadn't asked any questions, it was making me feel uncomfortable that he was there while a man was hanging in a nearby building.

At the sound of my voice, Jack got up and trotted over. I stroked his face and head. 'Hello, boy.'

'He's a beauty,' Sian remarked with a forced smile as she watched.

'Thank you. He really is. Don't know what I'd do without him,' I confessed, and then pointed to the floor. 'Lie down now, boy. There you go.'

Jack immediately lay down at my feet, resting his chin on the floor.

As I sipped my tea again, my eye was drawn to a long line of prescription drugs in small capsules under the cupboard closest to me.

Sian saw me looking at them. 'They're for Marcus,' she said by way of an explanation.

I gave her a quizzical look.

'His health has been bad off and on since he was out in the Gulf. Even though they won't admit it, he suffered from that Gulf War Syndrome. Everyone in his platoon did.'

'That must have been difficult to deal with,' I said empathetically.

'It was. Especially as the Ministry of Defence wouldn't pay out any compensation.' Sian sighed, but her sudden anger was obvious. 'They all went to court over it about twenty years ago. It went to the Welsh Assembly in Cardiff.'

This rang a bell. I was pretty sure that Annie had something to do with the Welsh legal team that approached the Welsh National Assembly and the Ministry of Defence to call for compensation for veterans.

'Wasn't the Honourable Justice Taylor involved in that process?' I asked.

Sian nodded as she put both her hands around her mug of tea as if trying to warm them. 'Yes, that's right. She was part of the commission. I liked her. But it didn't do us any good though did it? The MOD reckoned there was no evidence to show negligence on their part. Marcus said it was a cover up.'

I raised an eyebrow. 'He must have been very angry.'

'Too bloody right he was,' Sian said, but then her eyes drifted away and filled with tears. 'Sorry, I ...'

I remembered what that kind of shock and grief was like. A second or two of distraction before the crushing pain as the reality of what had happened took hold once again. It was exhausting.

'No, I'm sorry. I feel like I've been bombarding you with questions.'

Sian sniffed. 'Not at all. It's very kind of you to stay with me.'

Spotting a box of tissues, I got up, walked over and grabbed a couple and then handed them to her. 'Here you go.'

'Thank you.' Then she gestured over to Sam. 'If you and your grandson want to get off home ...'

I glanced over at Sam who was still engrossed in whatever he was watching on his phone.

'It's fine. My daughter is on her way over to pick him up. And I don't want to leave you here on your own,' I said. 'Plus, I went into that building. The police will want me to give a statement anyway.'

'Oh right. Of course,' she said, blowing out her cheeks and dabbing her eyes. 'You'd know about all that. How long were you a police officer?'

'Thirty-five years,' I replied, 'and twenty-five years in CID.'

I checked my watch. By my calculations, the police would be here any time. 'Shouldn't be too long now … How was Marcus yesterday and last night?' I asked.

'Fine. We were having such a lovely evening.' She sighed as she reminisced. 'Dinner. Few glasses of wine. Lit the fire and watched telly together on the sofa.' Then she looked directly at me with a furrowed brow. 'Marcus told me that it was perfect. Why would he say that if he was … you know? That doesn't make any sense, does it?'

'It doesn't.' I shook my head in agreement. But if there had been someone else involved in his death, then his behaviour would have been completely 'normal'. 'When was the last time you saw him?'

'It was 12.30am. Maybe a bit later. We'd decided to call it a night and head up to bed,' she explained tearfully. 'Marcus said he was going outside for a smoke. I don't let him smoke in the house these days. I went upstairs to bed. I'd had a few drinks so I must have just drifted off.' Then she took a deep breath to steady herself. 'I woke up and he wasn't next to me, so I started to look around for him.'

I gave her an empathetic look. 'Marcus never came to bed?'

She shook her head. 'No. I could see from the duvet

and pillows that he hadn't. That's why I was so worried. When he wasn't asleep on the sofa, I thought he might have had a heart attack outside or something.'

'Was there anything in particular worrying him? Anything going on that was bothering him?' If someone had killed Marcus and then staged it to look like suicide, there had to be a strong motive. I needed to know what was going on in his life in recent weeks.

'There's ...' Sian began to say something and then stopped herself.

'Sorry. I don't mean to pry,' I said gently.

'It's fine,' she reassured me. 'I'm sure the police are going to ask me all this when they arrive. Marcus had been suspended from school recently. A sixth form girl made an allegation about his inappropriate behaviour and language. But he told me that she had mental health issues, took drugs, and was generally a troublemaker. He said that the school had to suspend him and investigate, but his head teacher, Steve Collier, told him he was confident it would amount to nothing.'

'But he must have been worried?' I asked. My mind was already leaping ahead, wondering if his death was connected to this.

'Less than you'd think. His union rep was very helpful. Apparently, this girl has made false allegations before. To be honest, Marcus was more worried about her father.'

I gave Sian a questioning look. 'Her father?'

'Kevin O'Dowd. A right nasty piece of work. He'd been on social media, making threats against Marcus.'

I frowned. My mind was alert as soon as I heard the word 'threats'. A threat could mean motive. 'What kind of threats?' I asked.

'Oh, stupid stuff. That he and his brother were going to get Marcus because of what he'd done to his daughter.'

If my suspicions about Marcus' death were correct, there were already two people in the frame as likely suspects. And maybe Kevin O'Dowd and his brother had acted on the threats that they'd made against Marcus.

Out of the corner of my eye, I spotted two police cars pull up outside.

'Here we go,' I said to her.

Chapter 5

Fifteen minutes later, I was standing outside the farmhouse. Caitlin had just picked up Sam and Jack to take them home. A patrol car was parked outside and two uniformed police officers were now taking a statement from Sian inside. A CID car had just pulled up and, to my dismay, inside were DCI Dewi Humphries and DS Kelly Thomas.

My heart sank.

I had very little time for Dewi Humphries. In fact, I thought he was a pompous prick. He'd been a detective sergeant in the North Wales Police when I was over at St Asaph. We'd had several run-ins even though I'd been his superior officer. He was just one of those blokes with a huge ego who thought they knew everything and couldn't be told anything. I couldn't stand him, and I knew the feeling was mutual. Both Dewi and Kelly had been involved in the search for Meg, Annie's sister, three months earlier. For some reason, Dewi had done all he could to make my life difficult during the investigation even though I'd been retired from the force for fifteen years. However,

Kelly had been incredibly supportive so I was glad to see her at least.

Dewi was in his early 50s, with salt and pepper hair, a dark overcoat, scarf.

'Oh great. Happy bloody New Year,' he snorted sarcastically as he approached and saw me. 'What the hell are you doing here, Frank? You're like a nasty smell that just won't go away.'

Why don't you just piss off?

'Happy New Year, Dewi,' I said through gritted teeth. 'I'm surprised you've got time to come out here with that IOPC investigation hanging over your head.'

He bristled as he glared at me.

That'll shut your big mouth for a few minutes.

The Independent Office for Police Conduct – IOPC – was looking at an investigation into three murders in the late 90s in North Wales. A man named Keith Tatchell had been convicted of the murders at the time, despite protesting his innocence. Three months ago, it had been revealed that the murders had actually been carried out by Annie's husband, Stephen. I knew that Dewi and the senior investigating officer, DCI Ian Goddard, had cut corners and possibly fabricated evidence to secure the conviction of Tatchell. The IOPC was now taking a thorough look at the case again.

'In fact,' I continued, 'I'm amazed that you haven't been suspended pending the investigation.' Then I gave Kelly a half smile. 'Morning, Kelly.'

I heard Dewi mutter something under his breath. I didn't catch what he'd said, but I was glad that my little barbed comments had got to him. Fifteen love to me.

'Hi Frank,' Kelly said with a knowing look. I got the feeling that she wasn't Dewi's biggest fan either. But he was her boss. 'What are you doing here?'

'Me and my grandson were riding past when I saw Sian running from over there,' I explained, pointing to the stone building. 'I could see that she needed help, so I stopped to see if there was anything I could do.'

Dewi gave a little snort of derision. 'Very noble of you. Like a knight in shining armour, Frank? Is that right?'

I wasn't going to rise to him, so I looked directly at Kelly. 'She showed me her husband, Marcus. He's in that stone building so I checked it over.'

'Of course you did,' Dewi said, shaking his head. Then he looked at Kelly. 'I'm going to go and talk to the wife inside. Have a look up there, would you Kelly?'

Kelly nodded. 'Yes, boss.'

'And I'm sure that Miss Marple here would like to come with you,' he said in a withering tone as he wandered away. I don't think I remembered anyone getting under my skin as much as he did.

'Ignore him,' Kelly whispered as we turned and made our way across the neat garden. 'He's hungover. Heavy New Year's Eve.'

'I'm not sure that a hangover explains him being a total prick for the last twenty-five years,' I said with a wry smile, 'but thanks for the heads-up.'

The wind picked up and battered against us. I pulled the collar of my thick jacket up against the icy air. The thick branches in a nearby oak tree creaked with the force of the gust.

'What do you think?' Kelly asked me as she winced against the cold.

I laughed. 'Don't let Dewi hear you asking for my opinion.'

'Do you think he took his own life?'

I shook my head and looked at her dubiously. 'That's what I thought when I first went in there, but there's a couple of things that just aren't right. And I've been to my fair share of suicides over the years as you can imagine.'

Kelly beckoned for me to go into the building. 'Can you show me then?'

I had a lot of time for Kelly. She was calm, and had a wisdom beyond her years. I secretly wished that my own daughter could have been more like her. Together, sharp, and good at her job. It wasn't anything I would admit to anyone. It was hard enough admitting stuff like this to myself. I loved the very bones of Caitlin, and I'd do anything for her and Sam. And after what had happened to James, I knew how incredibly lucky I was to have my daughter and grandson in my life. They were so incredibly precious.

Walking slowly into the cold, dark interior of the building, I immediately looked over to where Marcus was hanging. Once again, I got a horrible flashback to finding James' body in the woods and then having to cut him down and carry him back to the farmhouse. I couldn't seem to get it out of my head.

I gestured to Kelly, trying my best to put those images of James out of my mind. 'He's over there.'

Marcus' body was swaying more than it had been when I'd been in there an hour earlier. The wind must have been swirling inside the building.

Kelly's voice dropped to a respectful whisper. 'It's horrible how you eventually get used to it.'

'Seeing dead bodies?' I asked, as I assumed that's what she was referring to.

'Yeah.' She nodded as she stared up at Marcus hanging from the central beam in the shadows. 'I wonder if it damages us permanently. Our ability to just switch off our emotions when faced with stuff like this.'

I was surprised at Kelly's openness and honesty.

'I don't think it can be healthy,' I admitted.

'No,' she agreed. 'Definitely not healthy.'

'Although at least these days you guys can go and speak to a counsellor,' I said. 'In my day, the solution to seeing a dead body or anything gruesome was seven pints of mild at the local pub.'

She gave a sardonic laugh. 'Yeah, there is that.'

Then I saw that the stepladder was now lying on the ground just beside Marcus.

'Bollocks,' I said under my breath as we went closer.

Kelly raised an eyebrow. 'Something wrong?'

'This stepladder was upright when I came in here earlier,' I said, taking a few steps forward and crouching down to look at it. My knees creaked a little.

'You think someone's been in here?' she asked.

'No.' I shook my head. 'I doubt it. It's only aluminium so its bloody flimsy. I guess that the wind blew it over. That's why he's swinging like that.'

Kelly looked at me quizzically as I stood up. 'And you thought there was something suspicious about it?'

'Yes. It was positioned right beside where his feet are now, but that handle at the top was in the way. There is no way that Marcus could have stepped off it with that rope around his neck without moving it or, more likely, knocking it over.'

Kelly gave me a sceptical look.

'I'm not making this up,' I said sharply.

'No. I don't think you are.' Then she nodded back towards the farmhouse. 'But I know someone who might think you are.'

I gave a groan. I knew she was probably right.

'I can show you, but I don't want to touch the steps just in case,' I said. Then I gave her a meaningful look. 'And there is something else.'

'Okay.' Kelly looked interested.

I leaned forward for a better view.

'Bollocks,' I said again under my breath. The clumps of mud that had been sitting on the top two steps of the stepladder had clearly been dislodged when it fell. Looking around, I saw that they had broken into smaller pieces and were scattered on the ground.

'What is it?' Kelly asked.

'When I arrived in here there was relatively fresh mud on the top steps of this ladder.'

'How do you know it was fresh?'

'I used the tip of a pen to test it,' I explained. 'It was moist. And it rained last night.'

Kelly looked impressed.

I shrugged. 'Trick from the old days. You can ask Marcus' wife, Sian, if she went up the steps last night but it seems very unlikely.'

'Yes, it does,' she agreed.

I pointed to the mud that was now scattered on the ground. 'Looks like the mud dislodged when the steps fell over.'

'You're sure about that?'

'Why would I make it up?'

Kelly nodded, but she looked confused by what I was saying.

As I stood up straight I gave the usual groan that comes with being seventy years old, and took a step towards where Marcus' feet were dangling.

'Thing is,' I said, 'there's no mud on the soles of these slippers. Well, certainly not enough to have left those traces on the steps.'

Kelly's eyes widened. 'Which means that there was someone else in here last night. And they went up that stepladder.'

'My instinct is that there was. The evidence is flimsy, but I know what I saw.'

A shadow fell across the room from the doorway.

It was Dewi.

'We can go, Kelly,' he said nonchalantly. 'I've just spoken to this man's wife. He's a teacher who's been suspended for inappropriate behaviour with a teenage girl. He was depressed and about to lose his job. Pretty cut and dried what's happened here. Uniform can deal with it.'

I looked at Dewi. That wasn't the picture that I'd got from Sian. But Dewi had already made his mind up that Marcus had hanged himself and they could now go and let the coroner deal with it.

'We think there might be some anomalies here, boss,' Kelly said tentatively.

'We?' Dewi's face fell. 'Jesus, Kelly. Has Miss Marple here started poking his nose in again?'

'No, boss. But there are a few things that don't quite add up,' Kelly said. I could see that she wasn't confident enough to go further.

'Put it in your report, Kelly,' he snapped.

'Dewi, you really do need to take what I found earlier seriously,' I protested as I walked towards him angrily.

He squared up and puffed out his chest.

Oh, here we go!

'Do me a favour, Frank,' he growled in a patronising tone. 'Toddle away home. You've got enough going on with your wife, daughter, and grandson. We don't need you playing amateur sleuth here just because you're retired, bored, and have nothing better to do.'

The desire to punch Dewi in the face was overwhelming, but I didn't fancy being taken to the cells. One day, though. One day, when he least expected it.

He sighed. 'Come on, Kelly. We've got some actual crimes to solve today.'

Kelly gave me an apologetic look as she and Dewi walked out of the building.

I followed them outside.

The sky above was now a battleship grey.

I watched them walk towards the two PCs to talk to them and then head for their car.

Then I wondered what my next move should be.

I wasn't about to ignore what I'd seen. And my fond memories of Marcus made me determined to find out what had happened to him. But I probably needed some help.

Maybe Annie was at a loose end. If I was right, she already had a connection to Marcus from the compensation claim.

Chapter 6

It was late afternoon, and I stood resting my arms on the wooden fence of the paddock up at my farmhouse. My mind was still a little pre-occupied by Marcus Daniel's suspicious death and Dewi's refusal to even consider what I had to say.

Watching Sam sitting astride Lleuad, I tried to put it out of my mind. I could see how much progress Sam had made in recent weeks. He was a very determined boy once he set his mind to something. Maybe even a little obsessive. And in that way, he reminded me of James. An obsessive nature which meant that logic often went out of the window.

'That's it, Sam,' I shouted over encouragingly as I saw his gloved hands holding and manipulating the reins with gentle confidence. 'Thumbs up, fingers curled around, little finger goes under. Imagine you're holding two mugs of tea.'

He turned towards me and grinned. He liked my little analogy.

Over to my right, Duke was grazing on some hay at the

far end of the paddock. I remembered when I'd first got him. He was so wild that you could have heard him half a mile away, neighing, bucking, swerving and crashing around. I wondered what the hell I was doing taking him on. Rachel thought I was mad. I'd heard of a local man, Charlie Torrance, who *had a way* with horses.

I'd phoned him up and he'd agreed to come down and see what he could do. I remembered him arriving. His weathered face, silver hair, and piercing blue eyes. He leaned on the rail by the paddock watching Duke roaming around for over half an hour. Then I watched in amazement as Charlie worked his magic. A mixture of reassurance and repetition. He didn't go chasing after him. He simply watched as Duke snorted, bucked, and raced around. He said the odd word. Eventually, Duke was done. He was tired, fed up, and covered in sweat. So he just stopped, scuffed the ground, and then stared quizzically at Charlie. It was as if he was wondering who the hell this old man was and what he was doing. For a good fifteen minutes, Charlie and Duke just stared at each other. Then Charlie turned and said, 'Come on, boy,' and with no hesitation, Duke just followed him across the paddock. The transformation was staggering. I'd never seen anything like it. And it was the best fifty quid I've ever spent.

It had taken over two hours, but Duke was like butter. For the first time, I was able to stand in front of him and stroke and nuzzle him. 'You see, Frank,' Charlie said, 'it's just about watching them carefully. That's all it is. Then you can see what they need.'

I glanced at my watch.

'Five more minutes, Sam,' I called over.

He pulled a disappointed face. He'd spend the rest of the day riding if he could.

I had four more days' holiday before I had a couple of

days' work as one of the Park Rangers at the Eryri/Snowdonia National Park. There were a couple of dry stone walls that needed rebuilding for starters.

The tops of my ears burned with the strong, icy wind. I tilted my head and looked up. The clouds were thick and grey and whipped overhead like a film in fast forward. The wind was shifting to the south, and that brought the arctic air spiralling down from the mountains.

I wanted to go inside, build a log fire, and play a game of Scrabble or watch an old movie. Rachel and I had sat and watched *Casablanca* together on Christmas Eve. She'd remembered that both Humphrey Bogart and Ingrid Bergman were the stars. And when Sam had started to play and sing *As Time Goes By*, Rachel and I had sung along. I treasured those moments with Rachel more than I ever had. And, if I was honest, I kicked myself for not cherishing or appreciating that type of thing when we were younger.

My thoughts then drifted away to the nagging doubt I had about Marcus' death. And I knew that wouldn't go away until I found out what had happened to him and why.

'Here you go, Taid,' Sam said as he tossed me the reins and put his hands on the pummel of the saddle.

He threw his leg over and dismounted expertly. I was so proud of him.

For a few seconds, we walked in silence as we led the two horses back up the pathway to the stables. The cold air was thick with the smells of hay, woodchips, and the damp heather of the land around us.

'They've said it might snow,' I said.

Sam beamed at me. 'Cool!'

'Have you ever built a snowman?'

He shook his head. 'No.'

'That's our first job if we get enough snow,' I said enthusiastically. 'I can't have you growing up never having made your own snowman.'

'Taid?' he said quietly as if he hadn't been fully listening to me. 'Can I ask you a question?'

'Of course you can mate,' I replied. 'You can always ask me anything. I'm your Taid.'

'That place we stopped at this morning. Did a man kill himself there?'

His question took me by surprise, but I wasn't about to lie to him.

'Yes, I'm afraid so. A man called Marcus.'

'Why did he kill himself?' he asked as I opened the wooden doors to the stables.

I looked at him as I ushered Duke into his stable. 'I think he was very sad,' I said gently. Now wasn't the right time to say that I thought his death was suspicious.

Sam closed the bottom half of the stable door. 'Why was he sad though?'

I put my hand on his shoulder, and we turned to head out of the stables and back towards the farmhouse and annexe. 'I don't really know. I think there were a lot of things in his life that were making him sad.'

'Didn't my Uncle James kill himself too?'

His question took the wind out of my sails for a moment.

I stopped and crouched down a little to look him in the eyes. 'He did,' I replied quietly. 'How did you know that?' I couldn't remember ever having discussed James in front of Sam. I just thought he was too young to try and understand what had happened.

'I overheard you and Mum talking over Christmas,' he said, and then pulled a face. 'Sorry.'

Maybe he had sensed my uneasiness.

'It's fine, mate,' I reassured him. 'You don't need to apologise. But yes, your Uncle James did take his own life nearly ten years ago.'

He looked completely baffled. 'But why?'

'He had a lot of problems. And he was very sad too,' I tried to explain.

Sam furrowed his brow. 'But why was he sad? He lived here with you and Nain, didn't he?'

'Yes, he did. And I don't know why he was so sad,' I said, my voice filled with emotion. 'I wish I had known why so I could have helped him more. But I just couldn't.'

Sam looked directly at me. Maybe he could see that I was getting upset. 'Doesn't that make you and Nain sad?'

I nodded and took a deep breath. 'Yes, it does sometimes. It makes us very sad that we couldn't help your Uncle James.'

We looked at each other and I reached out to give him a hug.

'You're very precious to me, you know that?' I said, as my voice lowered to a whisper. 'And if you ever need to talk to someone, I'm always here. Don't ever keep things to yourself, okay?'

He nodded pensively.

'Everything alright?' asked a voice.

It was Caitlin.

'We were just talking about Uncle James,' Sam told her in a soft voice. 'Taid said that what happened to him makes you all sad.'

'It does. Very sad.'

Sam shivered and his teeth chattered a little.

Caitlin pointed towards the annexe. 'Why don't you go and get into the warm, Sam. It's flippin' freezing out here.'

He pulled a disapproving face. 'You're not allowed to swear, Mum.'

I stifled a laugh.

Caitlin grinned. 'Erm, I don't think flippin' is a swear word, but I won't say it again.' Then she pointed over to the annexe. 'Maybe make us some hot chocolate, Sam? I just need to talk to Taid.'

'Okay,' he said as he turned and jogged away.

'Little bugger,' Caitlin laughed, but then she spotted my face. 'You okay, Dad?'

I gave a little shrug to suggest that I probably wasn't. 'Seeing Marcus this morning. It brought everything back with James. It's knocked me for six if I'm honest, love.'

She reached out and put her hand on my arm. 'Of course it has. It's bound to have upset you.'

'What did you want to talk to me about?' I asked, feeling uncomfortable and wanting to change the topic of conversation.

She held out a yellow post-it note. It had a mobile phone number written on it. 'This number has called my phone a couple of times. No message though. I've checked and it's not spam.'

I gave her a concerned look. 'You think it's TJ?'

She nodded. 'Yeah.'

I took the post-it note. 'Leave it with me. I might be able to use this to track down where he is. Come on, I'm getting cold.'

We turned to walk back towards the farmhouse and annexe. I made a mental note to contact Annie as soon as I got inside.

Caitlin looped her gloved hand inside my arm as we walked.

'And how are you going to find out where he is just from a mobile phone number?' she asked suspiciously.

I tapped the side of my nose. 'Not just a pretty face, you know?'

She laughed.

'And keep the bloody doors locked when you're in there,' I said sternly.

'Maybe I should have a shotgun,' she suggested.

I thought for a second. 'That's not such a bad idea actually, but I'd need to teach you how to shoot it first.'

'You taught me how to shoot when I was fourteen, Dad.'

Chapter 7

Annie got out of her car and immediately felt the icy wind. She buttoned up her coat to the top and pulled on her fleece-lined leather gloves. She'd managed to find a parking space in the middle of Corwen. It was New Year's Day so most of the shops were closed. However, she'd managed to find flowers, a box of decent chocolates, and a bottle of Prosecco on the way. It had been ten years now that she'd been visiting her daughter Meredith and grandson Ethan at their flat in the centre of town. Ethan still had no idea that Annie was his grandmother – or Nain in Welsh. She knew the reasons why Meredith didn't want to tell him. Ethan had had a difficult start in life. His father had left when he was very small, and then he'd found himself getting into trouble at school and then with the police. Meredith didn't want to burden him with any more emotional baggage. It made Annie sad that she couldn't be completely honest with Ethan about who she was, but she had to respect her daughter's wishes. She was just grateful to have them in her life. It was such a joy.

As she made her way towards Meredith's flat, she

spotted The Berwyn Arms pub. With its whitewashed walls and black wooden window frames and doors, the pub dated back to the 17th century. Annie had a different reason for having fond memories of the pub. Back in the 1970s she, and her friend Gaynor, had been huge fans of the American actor, Al Pacino. Their favourite film was *Serpico*, which was the true story of a New York detective who became a whistleblower on the widespread police corruption in the city at the time. Having reported the rampant corruption to senior officers, Frank Serpico realised that his findings were continually swept under the carpet. Eventually he went to the *New York Times* who ran the story. As a reprisal, he was lured by fellow police officers to a drugs raid where he was shot but survived. As a result, Frank Serpico became Annie and Gaynor's hero as a brave, honest, cop who refused to accept the culture of corruption. When Serpico left the NYPD he travelled throughout Europe. And in 1979, Annie and Gaynor received the incredible news that he was living in Corwen. One night, they sought him out in The Berwyn Arms where they'd heard he used to drink. Having got his autograph, Serpico asked them to join him for a few drinks and they spent the evening talking and drinking. It was a night that Annie would never forget. It was also the pivotal moment where she decided to pursue a career in criminal law and hold those in authority, who were corrupt or abused their power, accountable for their actions. It was something that she had been passionate about, especially when she worked as part of a legal team investigating the systematic sexual abuse of boys in the care homes of North Wales in the 1970s and 1980s.

Annie crossed the road and went to a door that was adjacent to a sandwich shop with a bright red frontage. Once in a while, she'd pop into the shop when visiting.

They made the most incredible sandwich of smoked salmon, egg mayonnaise, spring onion and chives – with plenty of black pepper and lemon juice. As far as she was concerned, it was the best sandwich on the planet.

Looking down at her phone, she saw that she had a missed call from Frank. Then a text from him: *Hi Annie. I need to ask you a favour. You about for a call later? F x*

Annie messaged him back to say that she would call when she was back at home.

Putting away her phone, she then pressed the buzzer and Ethan came to the door.

'Happy New Year!' she said, giving him a hug.

'Yeah, Happy New Year,' he laughed, hugging her back. He smelled of shower gel or aftershave. Ethan always smelled so clean as if he'd just walked out of a shower.

He let her in and led her up the stairs.

'How was your New Year's Eve, Ethan?' she asked.

'Quiet. Very quiet,' he said with a little laugh. 'That's the way I like it these days.' He looked at her and grinned. 'I'm getting old, you know.'

Annie chortled. 'Bloody hell, Ethan. What year were you born?'

'1991,' he replied. 'A long time ago.'

'1991?' Annie snorted with a wry smile. 'Yes, well as an old colleague used to say to me when I was a young barrister, *You're barely dry darling.*'

He pulled a face and laughed. 'Yuck. That's a phrase I won't be using any time soon.'

'No.' Annie chortled as she gestured to a bedroom door. 'Is she awake?'

'Yeah. I've just taken her toast and tea like the dutiful son I am.'

Annie gave him a smile. 'You're a good boy, aren't you?' Then she knocked on the door and opened it.

Meredith was sitting up in bed drinking her tea. She had a beautiful, green floral-patterned scarf wrapped around her head to hide her hair loss from the chemotherapy.

'Happy New Year,' Annie said as she went over and gave her daughter a hug.

Meredith kissed her on the cheek. 'Hey, Mum. Ooh, you smell nice. What are you wearing?'

'Clean socks?' she joked.

Meredith giggled as Annie sat down on the edge of the bed.

'Did you see in the New Year?' Annie asked.

'Oh yes,' Meredith said dryly. 'Big bag of coke, couple of pills. There I was, up on a podium, throwing shapes to some bangers. Fuck me, I've only just got in.'

They both laughed.

'Take that as a no then,' Annie said with a smile.

'Asleep by ten.'

Annie laughed. 'Me too. Rock'n roll.'

'Still okay to take me next week?' she asked.

'Of course.'

Meredith had an appointment at oncology at Glan Clwyd Hospital to see if the latest round of chemotherapy had been successful. It was an anxious time having to wait for the results.

'Is it in the diary on your phone, Mum?'

Annie gave her a mocking frown. 'Are you trying to say that I'm getting forgetful in my old age?'

'Erm, yes.'

Annie noticed a pen and a notepad with a list on it on top of the bed.

'What's that?' she asked.

'My bucket list. I've just started it.'

'Oh my God, Meredith!' Annie said with a horrified

expression. 'You're not going anywhere. So, you can get rid of that.'

'Well I hate to break it to you, Mum, but I am going to die one day. We all are. Even you,' she said playfully.

'Well, that's very festive. I'm glad I popped over,' Annie joked.

'No harm in having a list of things I'd like to do before that day comes.'

'I suppose not. What's top of the list?'

'Have sex with Tom Hardy,' she quipped.

Annie shook her head. 'Ambitious, but I'm with you on that one.'

'Mum!' Meredith said with a look of mock disapproval.

'Seriously. What have you written down?'

'Taj Mahal, and not the one on Bala High Street that does a great Chicken Madras.'

Annie chortled. 'No, I know … I think that would be on my list too. A friend of mine told me that the Taj Mahal was the only place in the world she'd visited that actually took her breath away and was more extraordinary than any photo could show.'

Meredith thought about that for a moment. 'You've just downsized. You can take me.'

'Deal,' Annie laughed. 'Why not?'

Then her phone buzzed with a message. It was from Frank.

Meredith raised an eyebrow. 'Anything or anyone interesting?'

'Just a message,' she replied in a nonchalant tone.

Meredith frowned, her interest now piqued. 'From?'

Annie tapped at her nose. 'Never you mind.'

'Mum?'

'It's from Frank Marshal. Probably wishing me a Happy New Year, that's all.'

'Frank Marshal, eh? The handsome, silver haired ex-copper who thinks he's a cowboy?' she asked with a knowing look.

'Yes. That Frank Marshal,' Annie answered defensively.

'Right.' Meredith's eyes lit up with interest. 'Are you and Frank …?'

Annie shook her head. 'No. We're just very good friends. I've told you before.' Then she gestured to the door. 'Fancy another cuppa?'

'Trying to get away?' she teased, and then pointed. 'Anyway, you've got a bottle of Prosecco in your hand.'

Annie glanced at her watch. 'Bit early, isn't it?'

Meredith sighed and then grinned. 'Oh God, Mum. It's New Year's bloody Day. Live a little. I might not be here for the next one.'

'I wish you'd stop saying stupid things like that,' Annie growled.

Meredith smirked and then pointed to the door. 'Go and get us some glasses then, would you?'

Chapter 8

It had been half an hour since I'd picked up Annie, who had agreed to help me. Despite talking to her last night, I filled Annie in on the events of the previous day again, but this time in more detail. The early morning sunshine had burned away the clouds, and I could tell it was going to be one of those icy, clear blue Eryri/Snowdonia days that I loved so much. Perfect for a long horse ride or hiking up into the mountains. Except I had a possible murder to solve, so everything else was put on hold until I could find out what had happened to Marcus.

Annie glanced across at me, a smile tugging at her lips. 'You really do like country music, don't you?'

She was referring to my taste in music. *Slow Burn* by *Kacey Musgraves* was playing.

'You make it sound like I'm in some satanic cult,' I quipped.

She laughed. 'No. I think it's very endearing.'

'Endearing? Are you patronising me, Annie Taylor?'

'Erm, maybe. A bit.'

'Anyway, I'll have you know that country is now cool,' I

joked. 'There was something about it in the papers the other day. The kids love it.'

'The kids, eh?'

'Yeah. Gen Z or whatever we call them. They're all into country music.'

She raised an eyebrow dubiously. 'Okay, Hank,' she joked. 'I believe you. If you want to be 'cool', knock yourself out.'

'I don't think I've ever been cool. I was too young to be a hippy and into free love. Then I was far too old to be a punk. I got stuck with all that prog rock stuff in the early 70s. Peter Gabriel has got a lot to answer for.'

'Disco?' she teased.

I laughed. 'Not a big disco scene in North Wales back in the day. Plus, I couldn't squeeze into tight disco pants or balance on silver platforms.'

'Yes, that was glam rock,' she corrected me.

'Oh, right.' I pulled a face. 'T Rex?'

'Yes. Slade, Wizzard.' Then she shook her head. 'My friend Sharon Peters made me go with her to a Bay City Rollers concert in Liverpool in the early 70s. I don't think my ears have ever recovered from all that screaming.'

I smiled and then looked up at the direction sign as we took the turning for Bontnewydd, which was Welsh for *New Bridge*. It was a small village just south of Caernarfon, close to the river Gwyrfai. It was where Marcus' father Richard Daniels lived. I knew how difficult it had been for him nursing his wife Indira after she'd had a major stroke. I'd visited them on several occasions. I felt I owed it to Richard to see him and tell him that I'd seen Marcus yesterday morning. I also wanted to flag up that I thought there were suspicious circumstances, despite what North Wales Police, and specifically DCI Dewi Humphries, thought.

As I pushed the accelerator, I felt the engine of my pick-up labour a little. I knew it was time to trade 'her' in. I'd had my eye on a Ford Ranger pick-up for a while now. And of course, I was drawn to any truck with the word 'Ranger' in it.

Annie looked lost in thought as she gazed out of the passenger window. It wasn't surprising after all she'd been through in the past three months. I still had flashes of fighting with her husband Stephen, and Annie stabbing him.

One of the reasons I'd asked her to come with me was that I didn't like the thought of her rattling around her new house on her own. I knew she had friends, but selfishly I enjoyed her company. If I was honest, since Rachel's descent into dementia, I looked forward to my conversations with Annie.

'How are you settling in?' I asked.

She replied without looking over at me. 'I'm not.'

There was an awkward silence.

Then she turned towards me.

'Sorry,' she said. 'I was in the other house for over thirty years. In the space of three months I've lost my sister, nephew, and husband, with all the horror and pain that comes with that. And I had to move out of my home. It just takes a lot of getting used to.'

'Of course,' I said sympathetically. 'I'm always at the end of the phone. Anytime. And we've got that spare room if you just don't want to be on your own.'

'The front door doesn't even fit properly,' she groaned. 'It rattles in the wind. Funny how the estate agent forgot to mention that.'

'I'll come over and have a look. I'll rehang it, or we'll get you a new door.'

Annie smiled at me and our eyes met. She shook her

head and smiled. Her whole face lit up when she smiled. 'Underneath that rugged exterior you're a bit of a softie, aren't you, Frank?'

I grinned back at her. 'Rugged exterior, eh?'

'Come on,' she chortled. 'You're Snowdonia's answer to Clint Eastwood.'

'Well, I'll take that,' I said, but I was uncomfortable receiving any compliments. I always had been.

I glanced up and saw a sign that read *Bontnewydd*.

'Here we go,' I said as I peered over at the satnav. I was sure the place names and roads were getting smaller every time I looked at the digital map. Either that, or my eyesight was deteriorating.

'What's Richard Daniels like?' Annie asked as I turned into a residential road.

'Lovely man …' I replied, but then I hesitated.

'What is it?'

'Oh, it's just that he had a bit of a reputation back in the day. Eye for the ladies. Bit of a philanderer,' I explained, but then felt guilty about gossiping about a man who had just lost his son.

'I thought you said he was married?' Annie asked with a frown.

I shrugged. 'It was the 70s. You remember it was all a bit different back then. But Richard is a nice guy and he'd do anything for anyone. That's why I felt I should come over and see him.'

'I've realised that I met Marcus Daniels when I was part of the legal team that looked at their compensation case against the MOD.'

'Gulf War Syndrome?'

'Yes. The Welsh Assembly refused to take it any further, but it was the bastards at the MOD who just did everything in their power to destroy the case. They were definitely hiding something.'

'You think there was a cover up?' I asked.

'Absolutely. My instinct was that there was something very fishy going on.'

I scratched at my chin. 'What about Marcus?'

'He was their main spokesman. He seemed like a genuine bloke. Articulate, very passionate, and he really cared about all the veterans who had suffered after that conflict. He was devastated when the case was dropped.'

I nodded as we parked up outside Richard's address.

'When James was at the school where Marcus taught, I only ever heard good things about him. And I remember Marcus being very warm and encouraging when it came to James' work. It just makes me wonder why someone would want to murder him and try and pass it off as suicide,' I said as I took off my seatbelt and opened the driver's door.

We got out and made our way up the garden path which was still a little icy. The garden was neat and well tended, with a brush of frost across the lawn. It was bordered by a dark green privet hedge and a low brick wall that was covered in moss and lichen. The flower beds were populated with rose bushes. Nearby, large sprawling rosemary bushes, with their branches of mauve flowers, hung over the paved pathway. The air was thick with the smell of them.

As we reached the front door, I gave it a knock and took a step back. There was a thick front door mat that had *CROESO* – Welsh for Welcome – printed on it in ornate black lettering. There were cute little hanging baskets either side of the door that swayed a little in the cold breeze.

Annie wore a fetching cream ski hat, gloves, and a cashmere scarf. She was always immaculately dressed. She stamped her feet from the cold as her breath froze on the icy air.

After a few seconds, the door opened slowly.

A portly man in his 70s, glasses, balding, thick burgundy cardigan, peered out at me. For a moment, he looked confused.

'Frank?' he asked.

'Hi Richard,' I said gently.

'It's good to see you, Frank,' he said under his breath, 'but this isn't a good time, mate.'

His face looked gaunt and grey, and his eyes were lost somewhere in his grief.

'I know,' I said in a reassuring tone. 'I was at Marcus and Sian's place early yesterday morning.'

'Were you?' He looked confused.

'I just happened to be riding past with my grandson when Sian found him,' I explained, and then my voice dropped to a whisper. 'I went in and saw him. I'm so sorry, Richard.'

He took a few seconds to process what I'd told him, then he opened the door wider. His arm shook quite violently as he limped to one side. By the looks of it, his Parkinson's had got a lot worse since the last time I'd seen him.

Richard looked at me and gestured. 'God, I didn't know that. Come in.'

FIVE MINUTES LATER, Annie and I were sitting on a big sofa in front of a roaring log fire in Richard's living room. The walls were covered in bookshelves, and posters from old art exhibitions and plays. There was a black upright piano in one corner.

Richard sat opposite us in a big leather armchair. He took off his glasses and tried to clean them. His hands were shaking which was making it difficult. 'Bloody Parkinson's,' he growled angrily. 'Sorry. Do you want a drink? Coffee, tea, something stronger?'

Annie looked at him compassionately. 'We're fine,' she said softly.

'I had two police officers here earlier,' he said as he sat back in his chair. He had a haunted look on his face. 'They were so bloody young,' he said with a half smile as he shook his head. 'I've forgotten that saying but it definitely did make me feel very old.'

I sat forward and interlaced my fingers. I wasn't sure how I was going to broach this. 'There's a reason I came over to see you, Richard. Not just because I was there yesterday morning.'

'Okay.' He squinted at me, looking puzzled. 'You've lost me, Frank.'

'I went into that stone building where Marcus was,' I explained quietly. 'My instinct is that there was something suspicious about it.'

For a few seconds, it was as if he hadn't actually heard what I'd said.

'Suspicious?' he then asked, peering over the top of his glasses.

'There were certain things that didn't add up.' I was aware that in my effort to spare him the horrible details of his son's death, I was making my explanation painfully vague.

'You're not making much sense, Frank.'

Annie gave me a look as if to say, *You need to tell him what you found.*

'I'm sorry. I know this is very upsetting …'

Richard rubbed his face with his shaky hand. 'Listen

Frank, whatever it is, however terrible, you just need to tell me.'

'Marcus had used a stepladder,' I said, 'but it was in the wrong place. And there was mud on the steps that just doesn't match the soles of his slippers.' I looked directly at him. 'I think there was someone else there.'

Richard's eyes glistened with tears as he listened. Then he took a white handkerchief from his trouser pocket and dabbed at his eyes. 'Sorry,' he sniffed.

'Please don't apologise,' Annie said.

'It's just that I feel almost relieved that you've said that,' he said, staring into space. 'I know that must sound very strange.'

'It doesn't,' I reassured him. 'It doesn't at all.'

I knew exactly what he meant all too well. I had lived with my own son's suicide for nearly ten years. All the questions, guilt, and shame.

Richard sat forward. 'I was so shocked when the police told me this morning. I knew he wasn't happy … but if you think there's something not right, you should know, Frank. You were in the force for a long time.'

Annie crossed her legs. 'There were these allegations hanging over him at the school where he worked. I understand that he'd been suspended?'

'Yes, that's true, but he seemed very confident that it would amount to nothing. He'd told both me and Sian that he'd been assured by his head teacher that the girl was prone to making stuff up. But I thought he was just putting on a brave face. He could have lost his job.'

'If you could keep what we've talked about today just between us?' I asked. 'I'd like to raise my suspicions directly with Sian tomorrow if that's okay?'

Richard nodded. 'Of course. No problem.'

'What was his and Sian's marriage like?' Annie asked.

He took a moment and then pulled a face. 'I don't think they were happy. And to be honest, I think the marriage had been on the rocks for a few years now. Marcus was my son, but he brought a lot of trouble to their door. He just couldn't keep it in his trousers, if you know what I mean?'

I nodded. I knew exactly what he meant.

'What about this girl at the school then?' Annie asked.

Richard shrugged. 'To be honest, I don't know. She's seventeen and very pretty. I'd love to tell you that Marcus wasn't like that, but I can't.' Then something occurred to him. 'If you think that someone else was involved in Marcus' death, then maybe you should have a look at the girl's father.'

'We heard there had been some pretty horrible online trolling and abuse,' I said.

'It wasn't just that,' he stated. 'The father is Kevin O'Dowd. Nasty piece of work. He's the landlord at The Crown in the middle of Dolgellau.'

'I know it,' I said, although it was probably ten years since I'd been in there. I'd got out of the habit of drinking in pubs, the older I got.

'Marcus told us that Kevin and his brother Michael waited for him in the school car park before Marcus had been suspended,' Richard explained. 'Marcus didn't tell Sian. He didn't want to worry her.'

Annie raised an eyebrow. 'What happened?'

'Marcus thought they were going to attack him, but there were too many people around. But Kevin told Marcus to watch his back because he was coming for him.'

I shot a knowing look over at Annie. It sounded like we needed to take a good look at Kevin O'Dowd.

Chapter 9

Annie and I walked into The Crown pub. It was very old fashioned and slightly shabby. Red patterned carpets, dark wooden furniture, dim lighting. It smelled of cheap beer and fried food. There were a few ruddy-faced regulars drinking and chatting at the bar. They were probably drinking off their hangovers from the night before. They had that kind of look about them.

'I like what they've done with the place,' Annie said sarcastically under her breath.

'It has a certain charm,' I said with a smirk. 'I'm not a big fan of all these bloody gastro pubs, but this place looks like you might need a tetanus jab when you leave.'

She chuckled. 'Hey, they've got pickled eggs on the bar. I'm quite partial to a pickled egg.'

I pulled a face. 'Just when I think you can't surprise me …'

'I like to be unpredictable.' She gestured to the bar. 'How are we going to do this?'

'The problem with being a retired copper is that I don't

have a badge to flash so that I can start asking questions,' I pointed out.

Annie shrugged. 'I guess we have to be inventive then.'

A girl in her late teens - dyed red hair, pierced eyebrow - was wiping down a table nearby.

Annie went over to her. 'Excuse me. Can you point out Kevin for me?' she asked quietly.

The girl nodded and pointed over to a man on the far side of the bar with very short ginger hair and a beard. He was well built and looked like he could be intimidating. I guessed that was useful when you're the landlord of a pub like The Crown.

Annie beckoned me to follow her. 'Come on.'

'Right,' I said. I wasn't quite sure what she was up to.

'Hi there,' Annie said politely as she looked at O'Dowd and gestured to us both. 'We were in here on New Year's Eve for a while and I think I might have left my phone.'

O'Dowd gave us both a suspicious look. 'Erm, sorry love. I don't think we had any phones handed in. I'll just ask for you.' He looked at the girl. 'Beth? Anyone hand in a phone to the bar staff on New Year's Eve?' He had a very strong cockney accent.

Beth shook her head as she continued to wipe the tables.

I clocked that O'Dowd had a George Cross, a British Bulldog, and Millwall FC tattoos on his arms. As a proud Welshman, it didn't really endear me to him. In fact, it just reinforced the idea that I'd formed that he was a prick. And probably a racist prick.

'Sorry. Doesn't look like it, love.'

Annie sighed. 'Oh God, that's a pain. I bought some drinks at the bar about 11.30pm. You served me, and I know I had my phone then.'

'Couldn't have been me that served you, love.'

'Why's that?' I asked.

At the sound of my voice, one of the men on a nearby bar stool turned towards me with a quizzical look. There was something familiar about his lined, saggy, face but I couldn't place it. It was one of the downsides of working as a copper for so long in a rural area like Snowdonia.

O'Dowd gestured to the ceiling. 'Yeah, I was feeling a bit crook, so I didn't even see in the New Year. I went upstairs.'

'Aw, that's nice. So, you saw the New Year in with your wife?'

O'Dowd was starting to look a bit guarded. He frowned at Annie's question.

'Nah, my wife fucked off years ago.'

Annie offered him a bleak smile. 'Please don't tell me you were up there on your own?'

'Yeah, I was,' he answered with a note of finality. I sensed that he'd definitely had enough of talking to Annie. 'Anyway, sorry we haven't got your phone, love. And Happy New Year.'

With that he turned his back to us and wandered down the bar to chat to some of the regulars. He was clearly talking about us as they all looked our way after a few seconds.

'Shall we go?' I asked Annie.

'Please. I feel decidedly grubby,' she said with a forced smile as we headed for the doors.

'He doesn't have an alibi for the time we think Marcus was killed,' I said under my breath as we went out through the doors into the icy air and walked over to where I'd parked in the pub car park.

'No, he doesn't. Which is interesting,' Annie agreed.

I clocked that there was a large black CCTV camera

mounted on to the back of the pub which covered most of the car park.

'Oi!' shouted a voice.

I turned and saw that O'Dowd was marching across the pub car park looking angry. His whole body was like a wound coil, and his hands were clenched into fists.

'Oh shit,' I muttered.

Annie glanced up at me. 'I don't think he's coming over here because he's found my phone, do you?'

'No, he looks a bit miffed.'

'Miffed? I'm not sure 'miffed' does it.'

'No,' I agreed.

'I want a word with you!' he yelled. He was now about ten yards away. His face was screwed up like that of a bulldog.

'Why don't you get in the car, Annie?' I said under my breath.

She took a few steps towards him and smiled. 'Everything all right?'

What is she doing?

'Out the way, grandma.' O'Dowd sidestepped Annie and came towards me.

I clenched my fists and prepared myself in case he attacked me. Which seemed very likely.

'Are you okay?' I asked very calmy. I didn't want to get into a fight, but I was more than prepared to defend myself.

His nostrils flared and his chest heaved. 'You're a copper, aren't you?' he snapped.

I shook my head. 'Not for a long time,' I said as if we were having a nice, friendly conversation.

'Don't split hairs, grandad,' he snarled. 'What was all that shit in there? You two weren't in my pub on New Year's Eve. You would've stuck out like sore thumbs.'

'No, we weren't,' I conceded. 'I just wanted to know where you were.'

'Eh?' O'Dowd blinked as he tried to process this. 'What the fuck d'you want to know that for? It's none of your bloody business.'

'Does the name Marcus Daniels ring a bell?'

'Yeah,' he growled. 'What, are you his dad or something?'

'No, I'm not, but Marcus was found dead yesterday morning.'

'What?' O'Dowd was silent for a few seconds. He looked very confused. My instinct in that moment was that he had no idea that Marcus was dead, and this was news to him. Then he fixed me with a stare. 'What, and you think I had something to do with it?'

'Did you?' I asked, and watched as he reacted with an indignant rage. Even though he was about to go off like a bottle of pop, I wasn't scared. He was overweight, already breathless, and had had more than a few drinks.

'You fucking cheeky bastard!' he sneered. 'I'd knock you out if you weren't so old.'

I finally lost my patience.

'Don't let my age stop you, sunshine,' I said with a smirk. I couldn't help myself. He was a horrible prick who might have murdered Marcus. I was happy to take him down a peg or two.

'Oh right. Like that is it?' he said, raising his eyebrows.

'Frank?' Annie said worriedly.

O'Dowd laughed and turned to Annie. 'It's alright, love. He's got a big mouth and just needs to be taught a lesson. Even at his age.'

Watching his every move, I braced myself.

He telegraphed his punch – as most drunk car park fighters do. As his right fist swung towards my jaw I grabbed his wrist, and in a swift move pulled his arm round and up behind his back. At the same time, I kicked out hard against his left knee.

With his left leg now jarred, I moved in and threw him to the ground face down. I held his arm and began to twist hard.

He groaned, wincing with pain. 'Jesus Christ!'

'I'm going to need you to tell me where you were after midnight on New Year's Eve,' I said very calmly as I twisted his arm further.

'Ahh,' he yelped. 'I've already bloody told you! I was upstairs in my flat.'

'Well, I don't believe you,' I snarled, aware that Annie was giving me a disapproving look.

He gasped and flinched through gritted teeth. 'Ah, Christ, I was there. What else do you want me to say? Where the hell do you think I was?'

If I twisted his arm any further I'd dislocate his shoulder or fracture his forearm, and I didn't want to get arrested for assault.

'I think you were at Marcus Daniels' home.'

He was in agony, but shook his head adamantly. 'I wasn't. I swear. Jesus, you're going to break my arm!'

Dropping his arm to the ground, I looked over at Annie who widened her eyes.

'Come on, let's go,' I said, as I clicked the automatic locking system open and the indicators flashed.

I opened the driver's door, got in, and started the ignition. I began to reverse, spotting that O'Dowd had managed to get to his feet, clutching at his arm.

'No lasting damage,' I said nonchalantly.

Annie shook her head. 'All I can say is that I'm very glad you're on my side, Frank.'

Chapter 10

It was ten minutes later as we drove across Eryri/Snowdonia in silence. The sun had decided to show its face, and the liquid blue sky was peppered with small clusters of clouds. Over to our left – which was east – sheep were making their way across an undulating field to a steel feed stall. Beyond that, the landscape tilted up. A bold line of muscular ridges reared up 2,500 feet to a ragged line of mountains.

I was deep in thought. Even though Kevin O'Dowd had a strong motive to kill Marcus, I wasn't convinced. My gut told me that it just wasn't him.

Annie turned to me. She must have read my mind. 'What did you think of our ill-mannered friend at the pub?'

I frowned as I reflected on her question for a few seconds. 'If I'm honest, I'm not sure. My instinct was that when I told him Marcus was dead he genuinely had no idea. He was completely thrown. It's very hard to fake a reaction like that.'

'I agree, but I have seen some great actors over the

years in the dock.'

'True.' I sighed, wondering if I'd just been hoodwinked by O'Dowd. Was he that clever? 'And I do think it's suspicious that he felt unwell and left his own pub before midnight on New Year's Eve to sit upstairs on his own. He didn't look very unwell to me.'

'And that means he doesn't have an alibi for the time of Marcus' death.'

'I noticed that the pub car park has CCTV,' I said. 'If we get hold of that, we might even be able to see if he left the pub when he said he was upstairs.'

'But how do we get the CCTV?'

'I haven't worked that one out yet. It's not like the old days where I could just flash my warrant card.'

'More's the pity.' Annie looked down at her phone and began to scroll.

I reached over and turned on the car stereo. *Breathe* by *Faith Hill* started to play.

'Some of this stuff is horrendous,' she said.

'Not a fan of Faith Hill then?' I asked, gesturing to the stereo.

'No. This,' she said, pointing to whatever she was looking at on her phone.

'What is it?'

She showed me a photo of a young woman wearing lots of make-up and pouting. Her lips were swollen, and it looked like she'd had collagen implants. 'This is Layla O'Dowd. The girl who made the accusation against Marcus, and that lovely man's daughter.'

'She looks about twenty-five,' I said, shaking my head and feeling very old.

Annie sighed. 'Well she's seventeen, and I've been reading the online abuse that Marcus received over this allegation at the school.' She pointed to the screen of her phone. 'It's horrendous.'

'The beauty of the internet,' I said sardonically. 'Freedom of speech.'

'There is someone on here who regularly threatens to kill Marcus. His handle is @realwelshboy1999. He references the school, Layla, and some local places around here. He must be local.'

'Could it be Kevin O'Dowd?' I asked, thinking out loud.

'My instinct is that 1999 is his year of birth.' Annie glanced at me. 'That's in my limited experience of course.'

'Well I have no experience whatsoever, but that would make this person 23 years old.'

'Good maths,' she joked.

'Thanks. I did that without a calculator,' I quipped.

'Impressive. At your age.'

'Hey, you're older than me.'

She laughed. 'Fair point. It must be your daily Sudoku.'

'My daily what?' I obviously knew what it was, but I was happy to play up to my persona of the rugged uncultured luddite.

Annie looked at me suspiciously. 'Frank, tell me you know what Sudoku is?'

'A Japanese fish dish?' I said, teasing her.

'Very funny.'

'No, Sudoku isn't my thing. Nor crosswords. Probably good for you to do them daily though at your age.'

She tutted. 'I am regretting ever revealing my age to you.'

I chortled. 'I think you'd had one too many glasses of red wine at the time, and you let it slip that you were born in 1950.'

'As was the actress Cybill Shepherd,' she said with a

knowing look, 'and she dated Elvis which makes her very cool.'

'I didn't know that,' I said with a grin. 'Think we went off on a bit of a tangent there.'

'Big tangent,' Annie snorted.

'Richard mentioned that Kevin O'Dowd and his brother had waited outside the school for Marcus,' I reminded her. 'Maybe this person is O'Dowd's brother?'

'Possibly, but unlikely if he's 23.' Then Annie turned her gaze to me. 'I know someone who could help us find out though.'

'I guess we're going to Corwen then?'

Chapter 11

As we reached the outskirts of Corwen it was mid-afternoon. I looked up, and the sky seemed vast and endless. I called it *The Big Sky*. It was a phrase that originated in Montana in the US to describe the enormity of the sky over the flat Great Plains of that particular state. In my eyes, it applied as much to Snowdonia as it did to Montana.

There was something redolent and even mystical about the view and the light. I had recollections of the ghosts of my childhood and the ghosts of a more recent past.

The Big Sky was also the name of one of my favourite Western films that was made by legendary Hollywood director Howard Hawks in 1952. It starred Kirk Douglas. Hawks had made some of my all-time favourite films. The original *Scarface*, *His Girl Friday*, as well as classic Westerns such as *Rio Bravo* and *Red River*. I also loved Howard Hawks because his middle name was *Winchester* which I always thought had to be the coolest middle name in the world.

As a child, I'd been obsessed with anything to do with cowboys. I loved Roy Rogers, The Cisco Kid, and The

Lone Ranger. I waited eagerly every week for my favourite television programme, *Rawhide*, in which Clint Eastwood played Rowdy Yates.

I parked in the centre of Corwen and noticed that the town was busy. The air had become noticeably chillier as the light of the day was quickly fading. A couple in their 70s crossed the road just along from where we were standing. The husband reached out for his wife's hand to make sure that she got across safely. It made me think about all the times that Rachel and I had held hands just going for walk. I wondered if I'd ever do that again with her. I probably wouldn't, and the thought of it made me sad.

Annie must have spotted the wistful expression on my face. 'You okay?' she asked.

'Yes, fine,' I answered unconvincingly.

She followed my gaze and saw the couple now walking along the pavement away from us, still holding hands.

Then she looked at me as if she'd read my thoughts. 'That's very sweet. I hope they realise how lucky they are.'

'I hope they do too,' I said quietly.

She reached out and put a comforting hand on my arm. Then she pointed to a door that was adjacent to a nearby sandwich shop. 'Shall we go in?'

'Yes. Of course.'

Annie pressed the buzzer as we reached the door.

It opened, and Ethan looked out. He was mixed race, with short dreadlocks, a black hip hop t-shirt, trackies and trainers.

'Hey, hey. Back again already?' he said with a beaming smile as he gave Annie a hug. Then he shook my hand firmly. 'Come in guys. Come in.'

'As I said on my text, we need your help,' Annie said as we went upstairs to the flat. 'Is your mum asleep?'

'Yeah,' Ethan said quietly. 'She's on these painkillers that knock her out.'

'Tell her I was asking for her, will you?'

'Of course, no problem.' We followed Ethan down the landing to where his office was located. His manner was energetic and frenetic.

The office was a large room at the front of the flat that had a multitude of monitors, keyboards, hard drives and laptops. There was a framed Arsenal football shirt up on the wall.

Ethan sat down in a big padded swivel chair and pointed to the three screens that were set out across his desk. 'How can I help?'

'Frank and I are looking into what we think is a suspicious suicide. Marcus Daniels,' Annie explained. 'He had been suspended from the school where he taught for alleged inappropriate behaviour towards a seventeen-year-old girl. Naturally, there have been a lot of online threats against him. There's one person in particular who we'd like to take a look at. @realwelshboy1999. We need to find out who he is and if his surname is O'Dowd.'

Ethan nodded. 'Right, let me see what I can do.'

He started tapping away at the computer, paused to use the mouse, and then began tapping again. I was completely baffled by what he was doing. I thought back to when I'd been a detective in the 90s and the first word processors and then computers had started to arrive in CID. I'd been fairly resistant to doing the training so I could use them. As far as I could see, they were just electronic typewriters that could very slowly access a newspaper article or two. Since then, I've had to hold my hands up as technology has revolutionised police work in the last twenty-five years.

After a short while, Ethan sat back in his chair with a

satisfied expression on his face. 'Right. Dude's name is Adam Morris. I've got his IP address which locates him to Minffordd.'

Minffordd was a village situated between Penrhyndeudraeth and Porthmadog. I knew it mainly because it had two railway stations, one of which was for the narrow gauge heritage Ffestiniog Railway. Of course, I remembered when it was a fully functioning station back in the 50s and 60s. *I can actually remember steam trains.*

'Can we find an address?' I asked hopefully.

'If he pays taxes or council tax we can,' Ethan said, but a few moments later he frowned. 'No, he doesn't ... but he might have a vehicle registered there.'

'Okay,' Annie said.

'Bingo. Here you go,' he said, pointing to the screen.

Annie grabbed a post-it note and scribbled down his address.

'Anything else?' I asked.

'Let me dig around a bit.'

I sat forward and ran my hand through my hair.

Finally, Ethan pointed to the screen. 'Here we go. Adam Morris has a fairly impressive criminal record. Racially aggravated assault in 2007. Suspended sentence. Public order offence at a Wales football game in Cardiff. Membership of a banned far-right group, *The British Defence Force.*'

'Jesus,' Annie sighed. 'He sounds delightful.'

'Can you have a look at Kevin O'Dowd for us too?' I asked. 'He runs The Crown pub in Dolgellau, but I'm pretty sure that he originates from South-East London.'

Ethan continued to work his magic. 'Yeah, I've got him,' he said after a while. 'Born in Bermondsey, 23rd August 1978. He has a string of offences as long as your arm. Public order, assault, and affray going back to the late

90s. Plus he still has a PBO, a Public Banning Order, issued by the Crown Prosecution Service for football hooligan-related offences while watching England abroad.' Ethan tapped his finger on the screen. 'Here we go. O'Dowd was also a member of *The British Defence Force.*'

I looked at Annie. 'That's weird.'

'What a charming pair,' Annie said in a withering tone.

My instinct told me something wasn't right.

'It's far too much of a coincidence if these two men were both members of *The British Defence Force* in this area and didn't know each other,' I stated.

'You're right,' Annie agreed.

'What's the connection?' I asked, thinking out loud.

Ethan continued to type energetically. 'Let me just check something …' It was remarkable to me just how quickly he could read stuff on the screen, type in data, and then move on to something else.

Then he sat back and pointed to the screen again. 'I think I've found it.' This time there was a blue logo and a Facebook social media page. I knew what Facebook was. Rachel had a Facebook page and she'd helped me set up something a couple of years ago. But I had to admit, I hadn't looked at it since.

I peered at the screen. The page belonged to Adam Morris, but I was none the wiser.

Ethan ran his index finger down the screen to show us. 'This is Adam Morris' relationship status. He's in a relationship with Layla O'Dowd.'

Annie put her hand on his shoulder. 'That makes sense. You're a star, Ethan.'

'I aim to please,' he said with a grin.

I fished out the yellow post-it note that Caitlin had given me. 'At the risk of pushing my luck, can you see if you can get a triangulated hit on this mobile phone number?'

'I'll do my best, but it'll take a while. Leave it with me and I'll call you when I have something.'

'Thanks mate,' I said. 'Really appreciate all this.'

Chapter 12

Half an hour later, we entered the small village of Minffordd. I knew it from my work as a Park Ranger. There was the well-known Minffordd path that took walkers through the Cwm Cau where the Llyn Cau lake was situated. It was one of my favourite places in Eryri/Snowdonia Park. The lake was huge and dramatic, set in a deep glacial crater, and located at the bottom of Cadair Idris. The icy black lake was also said to be a prison for a terrifying Welsh water dragon who had been dragged there by King Arthur to protect local villages. The lake was supposed to be bottomless, and so the dragon was trapped for eternity.

'You think these men killed Marcus, don't you?' Annie said, breaking my train of thought as I slowed the car, looking for the turning to Morris' address.

I brought myself back into the present and nodded. 'They both have a very violent past. And in their eyes, their daughter and girlfriend was molested by a mixed-race teacher.' I glanced over at her. 'I'd be more surprised if they hadn't taken matters into their own hands.'

Annie furrowed her brow. 'Doesn't trying to make Marcus' death look like a suicide seem very elaborate for men like that? Why not put on balaclavas, wait until he was on his own somewhere and just beat him to death?'

Annie's uncertainty was valid. Men like O'Dowd and Morris rarely had the brains or guile to try to do something as sophisticated as that.

'I see what you're saying,' I conceded as we took a left hand turn down a narrow muddy track, 'but if we go back to the basics of all good detective work – motive, means and opportunity – then both men have all those. And we don't have anyone else in the frame at the moment do we?'

She shrugged in agreement. 'No, we don't. Not yet.'

I could see that she wasn't convinced by what I'd said, but my philosophy in detective work was to follow the evidence to start with. And the evidence showed Adam Morris making online death threats against Marcus.

The track down to the location we'd been given for Adam Morris was full of bumps and muddy potholes. We were close to the river, so there was a vaporous mist that hung in the air the further down the track we got.

We came to a clearing and saw two old dilapidated static caravans. To the side of one of them was an old rusty fridge, a bed frame, and a smashed up washing machine. There were two fire pits and a scattering of old-fashioned collapsible picnic chairs with coloured stripes that had been faded by the sun.

I pulled my pick-up truck over and stopped.

'Looks like the sort of place you'd come if you wanted to buy some moonshine,' Annie joked.

I smiled. It definitely had that 'red neck' feel to it. Scanning the area, I could see that there was no one around. Over in a covered cage, three black dogs – possibly Pit Bulls - barked and snarled at the mesh.

'Maybe you should stay in the truck, Annie.'

She gave me an indignant look. 'Why do you keep saying that to me? I can look after myself.'

I shrugged. 'Sorry, I guess I'm just a bit old fashioned.'

'You really are.' She smiled at me. 'You're an old-fashioned gentleman, Frank, and very protective of everyone around you. That's sweet, but I'll be fine.'

We got out of the warmth of the truck and ventured outside into the cold misty air. It smelled damp and musty.

Very loud music was playing from somewhere inside the nearest caravan. The bass seemed to be making everything shake with its vibrations. Then I got a very strong smell of marijuana in the air.

I looked at Annie and gestured to the rickety door. 'Shall we?' I asked, raising my voice over the music.

She crinkled her nose as the smell of weed got stronger. 'Why not.'

We approached, and carefully stepped over the empty beer cans, pizza boxes and other rubbish that lay strewn around.

I gave the door an authoritative knock and took a step back.

Out of the corner of my eye, I saw the orange curtain at one of the windows twitch.

Then the music stopped, and a few seconds later the door opened.

A young woman peered out at us. I recognised her as Layla O'Dowd from the photo that Annie had shown me on her phone. Lots of eye make-up, pierced nose, and dyed blonde hair with black roots. She was wearing a grey hoodie and trackies and had bare feet.

'You collecting for charity?' she asked in a croaky voice. Her eyes were glassy as if she'd been drinking or smoking drugs. I guessed it was the latter.

I wasn't quite sure what she meant. Maybe she was confused as to why two people in their 70s were knocking at the door.

'Erm, no. We're actually looking for Adam,' I explained calmly. 'Is he here?'

'Nah,' she replied, shaking her head. 'No, Adam ain't here.'

God, she is really out of it.

She went to close the door in my face but I put my hand up to hold it.

'But he does live here, doesn't he?' I asked in a friendly tone.

Layla clearly didn't like the fact that I'd held on to the caravan door.

'Look,' she snapped. 'I don't know who you are or what you want, but you need to fuck off, all right?'

I moved my hand and allowed her to slam the door.

'Frank,' Annie said under her breath. I followed her gaze and saw a man in his mid-20s running towards a filthy red quad bike.

Adam Morris. I recognised him from his Facebook photo.

'Shit,' I said.

Annie pulled me towards the pick-up truck. 'Come on.'

We broke into a jog, got in, and pulled on our seatbelts as fast as we could.

Turning on the ignition, I stamped down onto the accelerator and felt the tyres spin on the mud before we lurched forward in pursuit.

Morris pulled the quad bike around in an arc and headed up the bumpy track that we'd used earlier.

'Bloody hell,' I grumbled as I sped behind him. 'I was meant to be playing Scrabble in front of a nice fire today.'

'Oxyphenbutazone,' Annie said with a grin.

I frowned. 'Erm, what?'

She laughed. 'Highest score word you can get in Scrabble. 1778 points.'

'Bollocks,' I quipped.

'It is,' she insisted.

'No. Bollocks. My favourite word to use in Scrabble. But just a measly 16 points.'

Annie shook her head with a mock look of disapproval.

I nodded towards Morris who was bumping and swerving through the potholes as we approached the junction with the main road. 'Any idea what we're going to do if we do catch him?'

Annie furrowed her brow. 'Ah, yes. Slight flaw in the plan. We can't really ask him if he was at Marcus Daniels' house on New Year's Eve and if he had anything to do with his death,' she said sardonically.

'True,' I agreed dryly, 'although the very fact that he's done a runner is pretty suspicious.'

I looked up and saw that Morris had reached the junction and turned left. Once we were out on the main road, his quad bike wasn't going to be any match for my Toyota pick-up in terms of speed.

We quickly hit 50mph. Then 60mph.

'Jesus,' I groaned. 'What's he got. A Ferrari quad bike?'

Annie gripped the door handle with one hand as we careered around a long bend at high speed.

As we came around the bend, the road straightened out and I could no longer see Morris or his quad bike.

'Where are you, you little bastard?' I muttered under my breath.

Morris might have just pulled off into a field and could now be hiding behind a hedgerow.

'He could be anywhere,' Annie groaned.

I nodded in frustration.

ANNIE and I approached the caravan door again. The music was pounding but there was no sign of the quad bike or Morris.

I banged on the door with my fist. I could sense that I was losing my patience.

The door flew open and Layla glared at us.

'I thought I told you two to fuck off?' she slurred. She seemed even more out of it than when we'd knocked half an hour ago.

She went to slam the door in our faces so I put my boot in the way.

'Oi,' she snapped. 'What the hell do you think you're doing?'

'You told us that Adam wasn't in,' I growled.

'So what?' She shrugged, then pointed to my boot. 'Move your foot or I'll call the police.'

'Oh come on, Layla,' I snorted. 'You won't call the police. You've got enough drugs in there to sink a ship. I just want to know where Adam was between midnight and 1am on New Year's Eve.'

She thought for a few seconds as if it was difficult to recall anything from thirty-six hours ago. 'He was here. With me. We had people round for a party.'

'Can you prove it?' I asked.

'Yes I can,' she sneered. 'Wait there.'

She stormed off.

I gave Annie a quizzical look.

Then Layla came back with her phone.

She turned the screen to show me a photo of her, Adam, and others with grinning faces. Then she swiped to show me another.

At the top of the photo there was a time and date –

12.38am 01.01.2023.

'Happy?' she asked with an exasperated sigh.

'Well, I wouldn't say happy. But thank you, Layla. You've been a great help,' I said with a calm, slightly sarcastic voice.

I took my boot from the door.

She gave me the finger and then slammed the door.

Annie looked at me. 'Her parents must be very proud.'

Chapter 13

I pressed the lift button for the basement of Glan Clwyd Hospital. The metallic doors clunked shut and the lift jolted before making its journey down one floor to where the mortuary was located. I could see my reflection in the shiny metal of the doors. There was that familiar jolt of reality that the person looking back at me was not in their 30s but was a 70-year-old man with grey hair and a beard. In my head I was still 30, even if all the little aches and pains were evidence to the contrary.

'These old lifts make me feel claustrophobic,' Annie admitted quietly. 'I think it was after I saw some horror film where someone gets trapped in one. *Marathon Man* wasn't it?'

I shrugged. 'I'm not sure.'

'Oh God.' She pulled a face. 'That terrible scene where Laurence Olivier drills Dustin Hoffman's tooth.'

'I haven't seen it,' I replied.

Annie laughed. 'Well don't … not if you want to go to the dentist's ever again.'

The lift clunked and jolted a little.

Annie looked at me anxiously. 'Oh God,' she said quietly, 'I thought it was going to stop. Can you imagine?'

I pointed to the steel inspection hatch on the ceiling of the lift. 'Well, if we get stuck I'll give you a bunk up through that and we can make our escape that way,' I joked.

'Oh, that's just what I want,' Annie chortled. 'I'm a bit old to start recreating scenes from *Die Hard*.'

'I haven't seen that one either,' I confessed.

'What? It's a classic Christmas film. Machine guns, terrorists, explosions.'

'Yeah, sounds really Christmassy,' I said with a dry smile.

'Although nothing can beat *It's a Wonderful Life*. Now that is a great film. I always had a bit of a crush on James Stewart when I was a kid.' Then she looked at me in disbelief. 'Oh don't tell me that you haven't seen that either, Frank Marshal?'

I grimaced. 'Sorry, but no.'

'Dear God.' She shook her head. 'Have you seen any films?'

'*The Searchers, True Grit, High Noon.*'

'Aren't they all Westerns?' she asked suspiciously.

'Erm, I believe they are,' I said with a self-effacing grin.

She gave me a withering look. 'Actually, that doesn't surprise me.'

The doors opened and we stepped out.

'Looks like we made it down safely,' I teased her.

She reproached me with a little smirk. 'Don't mock me, Frank.' I enjoyed the witty back and forth between us. Sometimes I wondered if I enjoyed her company too much.

As we walked down the windowless corridor towards the morgue, the drop in temperature was marked. I had pulled a favour at the local coroner's office and arranged for us to go and see Marcus' body and discuss the preliminary post-mortem. I was hoping that the PM would flag up that he hadn't taken his own life, and that his death was suspicious. If that was the pathologist's verdict, then Dolgellau CID would have to take my concerns seriously.

As we arrived at the black double doors that led into the mortuary, I noticed that Annie looked a little upset. It wasn't surprising. The last time we'd been inside this mortuary was three months ago when we'd seen her sister Meg's body.

'Sorry, I should have thought,' I said gently. 'Do you want to stay outside?'

Annie knew what I meant, and shook her head. 'It's fine. Probably cathartic for me to go back in here actually.'

As we made our way inside, the cold air was thick with the smell of disinfectants and other chemicals. There were two large examination tables nearby, with a third on the far side of the room. The walls were tiled to about head height in pale celeste tiles, and some work benches and an assortment of luminous coloured chemicals ran the full length of the room.

Glancing around, I spotted Professor Gareth Fillery – late 60s, tall, greying hair – over by a body on a metal gurney. I'd known Gareth for many years, which was a huge advantage when it came to processing my request to visit the morgue. He would have seen my name and authorised it immediately. He was now the Chief Pathologist for the whole of North Wales. He was dressed in pale green scrubs, blue latex gloves, and a fetching red bandana with a Welsh Rugby badge at its centre.

'Professor Fillery,' I said.

'Yes?' Gareth turned, frowned, and then realised it was me. 'Frank, you old bastard,' he said with a huge laugh.

'Hello, mate ... This is my very dear friend, Annie,' I said with a nod towards her.

'Yes, we've met a couple of times on a formal footing. Justice Annie Taylor, isn't it?'

'That's right. Most people don't recognise me without my fetching wig on.'

'I was called to do a couple of expert witness appearances at trials you presided over,' Gareth stated.

The underlying buzz of fans and the air conditioning added to the unnatural atmosphere. The pungent smell of cleaning fluids masked the odour of the gases.

Gareth pointed over to Marcus' white cadaver on the steel gurney. 'What's your interest in this?'

'I happened to be passing just after this man's wife found him hanging near their home. I knew Marcus, and I'm friends with his father Richard.'

'I see.' Gareth narrowed his eyes and peered at me. 'I've seen that look before, Frank. Why are you really here?'

Annie gave me a look as if to say *he's good*.

I put my hands up defensively with a knowing shrug. 'Okay, you got me, Gareth. There were a couple of things that I thought were suspicious when I saw him. Stepladder wasn't in the right place for starters. It looked staged. Mud on the aluminium steps but not on his slippers. Just my instinct.'

'What did the local coppers say?' he asked.

'They weren't interested. In fact, my presence at the scene meant that they didn't really look properly.'

Gareth looked confused. 'I'm not with you.'

'A know-it-all DCI from Dolgellau,' Annie grumbled. Even though we hadn't talked about it in a while, Annie still blamed DCI Dewi Humphries for Meg's murder. Had Dewi investigated the murders in the late 90s thoroughly, the police might have caught her husband Stephen back then.

'Long story, mate, but he just doesn't like me,' I said.

'Then he sounds like an idiot to me.' Gareth beckoned us over to Marcus' body. 'I've done the preliminary post-mortem. It appears like a suicide to me.' He used his index finger to indicate the purple and black bruising around Marcus' throat. 'We've got what I would normally expect to see. This is the ligature mark just above the larynx. There's severe damage to the sternocleidomastoid muscle, a fractured hyoid bone, plus a petechial haemorrhage.' He then pointed to Marcus' hands and forearms. 'Plus, no signs of a struggle. No defensive wounds. And this was a relatively young and healthy man.'

Annie frowned. 'Are you saying that we're wrong if we think someone else was involved?'

I then saw that Gareth had noticed something. 'Actually, hang on a second.' He took a closer look before pulling over the powerful light.

'What is it?' I asked.

'I'm not sure yet.' He took a small steel instrument and began to inspect something on Marcus' neck, just below his right earlobe.

I gave Annie a questioning look.

Gareth's expression turned to surprise. He gestured to the skin where he had been probing. 'There is the tiniest little mark here on the skin. Can you see that?'

I squinted. My eyesight wasn't good at the best of times these days, but I saw what he was referring to and I recognised it.

'Isn't that a needle mark?' I asked. I'd seen enough dead addicts to recognise a needle mark anywhere.

He nodded affirmatively. 'That's what it looks like to me.'

Annie narrowed her eyes. 'Someone injected him?'

'As far as we know, this man wasn't an intravenous drug user or a diabetic?' Gareth asked.

'No. Not as far I know,' I replied.

'And there's nothing on the PM or his medical records to suggest that he was. Plus, it's a very strange place to inject yourself. Slightly awkward to get to.'

'What about the toxicology report?' I asked.

'That's the thing,' Gareth said, looking perplexed. 'Nothing. A decent amount of alcohol in his bloodstream, but nothing to suggest that he would have been unconscious.'

'Then I'm lost,' Annie admitted.

'Could be gamma-hydroxybutyric acid,' Gareth said.

'GHB?' I asked. It was a party drug. A sort of liquid ecstasy. But I knew that it had also been used as a date rape drug too as it incapacitated people very quickly.

Annie nodded knowingly. 'I've seen a couple of cases where GHB has been used in a sexual attack or a rape.'

'And it's almost untraceable,' Gareth explained. 'GHB has a half life of only 30 to 50 minutes. 'Within two hours, it's pretty much left the body.'

'So, Marcus could have been drugged and then hanged,' I said, thinking out loud, 'and there would be no trace of it in his blood or anywhere else.'

'Precisely,' Gareth agreed. 'It also means that we're going to have a hard time convincing anyone from CID that he was drugged.'

I sighed. 'Yeah, that's my worry.'

Annie looked thoughtful. 'How much does Marcus weigh?'

'Big guy. 210 pounds,' Gareth replied.

'There's no way that one person managed to drug him,

drag him over to that building, put a rope around his neck and then hang him,' she pointed out.

'It doesn't sound likely,' I agreed.

'There is something that might help you though,' Gareth said.

'Anything,' I said, feeling a little disheartened.

'The needle mark is positioned exactly over the carotid artery. It's pretty difficult to locate unless you know what you're doing.'

'What does that tell us?' Annie asked.

'It tells us that either your killer was medically trained …'

I raised an eyebrow. 'Or?'

'… or they were a professional killer.'

Chapter 14

By the time we left Glan Clwyd Hospital, it had started to snow. Slushy flakes fell onto the windscreen but then dissolved. *Am I Losing You* by *Countdown Nashville* was playing quietly on the stereo inside my pick-up truck.

'I'm pretty sure that I came to this hospital when it had just opened,' Annie said, looking out at the dreary grey and white buildings.

'Early 80s, I think it was,' I said as we pulled out of the car park.

'That's when we got the results of the fertility tests. I haven't thought about that for such a long time.'

She'd never discussed with me why she and Stephen didn't have children. I'd always thought it was medical rather than an active choice. And it wasn't my business to ask.

I wasn't sure how, or if, to respond to what she'd said.

Then I bit the bullet. 'Is that why you never had children?' I asked gently.

She nodded thoughtfully. 'Yes. Stephen was infertile, apparently,' she said with an ironic shake of the head.

'You didn't want to adopt?' I asked as we got onto the main road heading east. The sleet was getting heavier so I switched up the speed of the windscreen wipers.

'Stephen wasn't keen. The irony is that I resented him all that time for not allowing us to have children. In reality, he was hiding the fact that he was a cold-blooded killer. The worst thing in the world would have been to bring a child into our home. And the one saving grace of all that carnage of three months ago was that we didn't have children who would have had to deal with the aftermath.'

I nodded with an understanding look.

'And that's the dreadful, dark irony, isn't it?' she continued, clearly keen to get this off her chest. I didn't think that she had many people who she felt comfortable sharing stuff like this with so I was flattered that she trusted me. 'There was me resenting Stephen for having affairs or not allowing us to adopt.' Annie's voice sounded choked with emotion. 'What I should have resented was the fact that he'd murdered three perfectly innocent women in 1997.'

I shook my head. 'I'm not sure how you begin to process all that.'

She wiped a tear from her eye. 'Me neither. I just put a brave face on it.'

'That's understandable. Anyone would struggle losing a sister. Without all the stuff that happened with Callum and Stephen.'

She gave me a thankful smile. 'Thank you, Frank. It's good to get it off my chest.'

'Of course it is,' I said. 'Anytime.'

We sat in silence for a few minutes but I could see that Annie was deep in thought. In fact, she looked apprehensive.

'Actually, while I'm getting stuff off my chest,' she said

quietly, 'I've got a confession to make. I've been lying to you.'

From the tone of her voice I could tell that this was something serious. 'Okay.'

Her voice dropped to a virtual whisper. 'I've been lying to you about Ethan and his mother Meredith.'

'Have you?' I asked. I really had no idea what she was talking about or what the lie was.

'Meredith isn't an old friend of mine … she's my daughter.'

Wow. I didn't see that coming, I thought.

'Your daughter?' I asked gently with a frown.

'Yes. I got pregnant when I was seventeen. Just some stupid night with a local lad. He wasn't even my boyfriend. My parents went completely mad. It was the late 60s so it was a very different time. I gave my daughter up for adoption.'

I saw Annie reach to her face and wipe away tears.

'That must have been so difficult for you?' I said with empathy.

'It was,' Annie said, her voice breaking with emotion. 'I felt so incredibly guilty, but I couldn't see any other way out. I was trapped. I couldn't just go and live as a single mum somewhere, and my parents made it very clear that they weren't going to support me if I decided to keep my baby.'

I glanced at her. 'Did you stay in touch or …'

She shook her head. 'No, no. I wasn't allowed to stay in touch. Once Meredith had been adopted, that was it.'

'So, what happened?'

'When Meredith turned forty, she decided to try and find me. Both her adoptive parents had died by then. Ethan had been born, but his father had left them and disappeared. Meredith contacted the adoption agency and then they approached me.'

'Wow, that must have been a shock.'

'It was, but I was so incredibly glad to hear from her. I had to keep it from Stephen. I'd never told him, but I'd thought about Meredith every day since she'd been born. I just wanted to know that she was okay and that she had been adopted by a nice family.'

'And had she?'

Annie sighed. 'Yes, thank God. A lovely couple. Rita and Harry. We arranged to meet up. Meredith had so many questions. She was a single mother bringing up Ethan. I guess she wanted to understand why I'd given her away rather than live as a single mum. She wasn't angry, but it made me feel very selfish and guilty.'

'As you said, the late 60s was such a different time,' I said. 'It was unheard of to have a child if you weren't married. And single mothers were just shunned.'

'I do think she eventually understood that, and then she told me about Ethan.'

'Of course. Ethan is your grandson.'

Annie smiled at me. 'Yes. He is.'

'Does he know?'

'No, he doesn't. Meredith was uncertain about telling him but he's said a few things over the years. And he's a very bright young man. I wonder if he suspects.' Annie reached over and touched my arm. 'I just wanted you to know, Frank. I don't want there to be any secrets between us. My life has been full of too many secrets.'

'Thank you for telling me,' I said with a kind smile.

AS WE DROVE over the brow of the hill, the snow was starting to swirl and turn in the air. I had to slow down as it was getting difficult to see ahead of us.

'I used to love the snow when I was a kid,' Annie said, looking out.

I smiled. 'So did I. We used to get snowed in on our farm for days. No school. Snowballs and snowmen. Sledging down hills with old fertiliser bags. It was so exciting.'

Annie laughed. 'Now it's just a pain in the arse.'

'And we're more likely to slip and break a bloody hip,' I joked.

We drove in a comfortable silence for a few minutes, gazing out at the blizzard.

'I've been running through what Gareth told us earlier,' Annie said, breaking the silence.

'Me too. I'm now convinced it wasn't suicide.'

Annie looked over at me. 'And there were two people involved in his death.'

'Yes, but on the downside I'm not sure about O'Dowd and Morris. If they were going to seek revenge on Marcus, they would have come round with baseball bats, knives, and balaclavas. And they would have killed him viciously. Plus, Morris seems to have an alibi.'

Annie nodded in agreement. 'An injection of GHB into the neck takes intelligence and sophisticated planning. And that's definitely not Kevin O'Dowd.'

'No. Two words that have never been used to describe him.'

My phone buzzed with a message. I picked it up and looked at the screen. 'Message from Ethan.' I handed the phone Annie. 'Can you have a look for me?'

'Yes, given that you're driving,' she said sardonically as she fished out her reading glasses and popped them on.

Then she held the phone almost at arm's length to read the message.

I gave a wry smile. 'Think you might need to get your eyes tested.'

Without looking up, she flicked me the two-fingered V sign and peered at the screen.

'Ethan has found an address for that mobile phone number you gave him, TJ.'

'Where is it?'

'Tal-y-llyn.'

I nodded. Tal-y-llyn was a small hamlet right by Tal-y-llyn lake and close to the village of Abergynolwyn. The river Dysynni flowed out of the lake nearby and went all the way down to Cardigan Bay.

'There's a heritage railway there, isn't there?' Annie asked.

'That's right. Not that I've been.'

'Yeah, riding on old steam trains isn't really my thing. I'm not that old,' she teased.

'Want me to drop you home?'

She shook her head. 'No.'

'Sure?'

'What am I going to do? Sit with a blanket over my knees and watch a crime drama? No thanks. I'll stick with you.' She then gave me a furtive glance. 'After all, what's the worst that could happen?'

'Now you're tempting fate.'

'I don't believe in fate.'

'Okay. But I've got to stop somewhere on the way.'

Chapter 15

I looked over at the black Ford Ranger pick-up truck on the lot at Eddie Dixon's garage which was just outside Dolgellau.

'I've been promising myself one of these for years,' I said to Annie and Eddie.

Eddie Dixon was in his late 60s, bald, pointed nose, glasses, with a black ski hat pulled down over his head. I'd known him for many years, as his brother Phil had been a copper in the North Wales Police at the same time as me.

'Definitely an upgrade on your Toyota, Frank,' he said, rubbing his hands together against the cold. Even though the sleet had now stopped, it was icy.

'Yeah, well you would say that,' I chortled in a friendly tone. 'You're trying to flog it to me.'

He guffawed as if this was the funniest thing he'd ever heard. 'That's true.'

'3.2 litre engine, beefed up suspension,' he announced, 'and 600nm of torque. You could drive this thing up a bloody mountain.'

'Yeah, yeah. Save me the sales pitch and go and get the keys.'

He laughed loudly at the ease of the sale. 'Really? And you're happy with the trade-in on the Toyota?'

'I trust you, Eddie.'

He gestured over to a blue Portakabin. 'I'll just go and get the paperwork and the keys then.'

'Great,' I said as he wandered away.

Annie gave me a quizzical look.

'TJ knows what truck I drive,' I explained. 'I don't want him clocking me if we're sat outside or if we follow him.'

She nodded in agreement. 'Makes sense.'

Eddie returned with the V5 documentation and the keys.

'I'd better go and get my CDs out of the Toyota.'

'Or you could leave them in there,' Annie teased me with a smile.

TURNING OFF THE MAIN ROAD, I applied the brakes. They were far more responsive than those on the Toyota so I was still getting used to them. But the Ford Ranger was a far more comfortable drive, and the bigger engine was obvious on the few times I'd used the accelerator to overtake. We headed down a narrow road lined with small cottages that were flanked on either side by rough heathland and sheep. The light of the day was starting to fade. Spotting *Rose Cottage* at the far end of the row, I pulled over about thirty yards further up the road so as not to attract attention.

TJ's car was parked on a scruffy concrete driveway.

'Ethan knows his stuff,' I said as I pointed to the car. 'That's TJ's car.'

Annie then gestured to the roof where smoke was coming out of the chimney. 'And it looks like someone's home. What's the plan?'

'No plan yet. I just wanted to see where he was living. Makes me feel a bit better now that I know where the little fucker is.'

'Do you think he would actually try and harm Caitlin again?'

'I'm not taking any risks. And he mentioned that he wasn't prepared to go anywhere without Sam. That's worrying me too.' Reaching into my pocket, I pulled out a small magnetic car tracking device.

Annie glanced at it under lowered brows. 'What's that?'

'A tracker.'

'I don't suppose there's any point telling you that putting that thing on his car is highly illegal?' she said with an impish smile.

'Nope.' I laughed as I got out of the car.

Keeping my eyes fixed on TJ's cottage, I moved swiftly across the road.

Then I crouched down as best I could with my creaking knees, reached under his car, and secured the powerful magnet against the underside of the chassis.

I stood up, moved slowly away, and got back into my truck.

Before I'd even had time to settle back into the driver's seat, Annie spoke. 'We have movement.'

I peered over and saw TJ and a giant of a man in his 40s heading out of the cottage and getting into TJ's car.

I sighed with relief. 'That was close.'

'A little too close.'

I started the truck's ignition. 'Right, let's just see where he's going, shall we?'

Keeping my distance, we followed TJ back down the track and out onto the B4405, heading south.

I reached over to my small collection of CDs and selected *Waylon Jenning's Greatest Hits*.

As *The Chokin' Kind* played, I looked out at the landscape. To our left were grasslands and sheep, before a steep ridge up to the hills leading to Cadair Idris.

Annie stared at me, deep wrinkles forming on her brow. 'Why the obsession with country music?'

I thought for a few seconds. It seemed obvious to me. It was the most beautiful, lyrical, and perfect music in the world.

'It's white soul music. It tells the stories of the lives of poor rural 'folk'. Their dreams, tragedies, faith, betrayal, and love. For me, it feels as relevant to the poor rural people of North Wales as it does to the States. I identify with it.'

'Right.' Annie looked faintly amused. 'Well at least you haven't given it much thought,' she said dryly.

'Very funny.' I gave a self-effacing grin. 'You think I'm being pretentious, don't you?'

She chuckled. 'Not at all. I wouldn't expect a Welsh cowboy like you, Frank, to listen to anything else. I just didn't know you'd given it that much thought.'

Before we could continue, TJ indicated right and pulled off the main road.

I slowed down and did the same.

We took a small, steep, gravel track that led us deep into the dark woods that banked the road to the right.

Within thirty seconds, the canopy of trees above us had shrouded almost any daylight that was left. We were driving in virtual darkness.

'What the hell is he doing out here?' Annie asked under her breath.

'I've no idea, but I hope that whatever it is it's highly illegal and something that he can be put in prison for.'

I spotted that TJ had now put on his headlights.

Unfortunately, I knew that I couldn't do the same without drawing attention to our presence behind him.

He pulled over to the right and parked his car in a small clearing in the trees which looked like a makeshift car park.

I slowed the truck to a stop and observed.

TJ and the large man got out of the car and went around to the boot.

I turned off the ignition and glanced over at Annie. 'I'm going to have a closer look.'

She unclipped her seatbelt. 'Well, I'm not staying here on my own.'

We got out and gently closed the car doors so as not to make any noise. Then we made our way through the trees and the undergrowth to get closer to where TJ had parked.

Even though it was now dusk, the headlights from his car were bright enough for me to see what he and the man were doing.

TJ opened the boot.

He and the man stood talking and looking inside for about a minute.

Out of the corner of my eye, I spotted about thirty old tyres that had been deliberately stacked together at the far end of the car park. I had no idea why.

Then I saw TJ grab something from the boot and step away from the car.

He was holding some kind of submachine gun.

Jesus Christ!

Annie's eyes widened as she looked at me and pulled a concerned face.

TJ handed the gun to the man to inspect. He turned it over, held it up, and checked the various parts.

If I was to make a guess, it looked as if TJ was selling it to him.

Then they walked across the car park and stood about 20 yards from the bank of tyres. It didn't take a genius to work out what was coming next.

TJ loaded the gun and took off the safety.

Suddenly the air exploded with noise as he shot several bursts of gunfire into the tyres.

The clattering noise of the bullets hammering into the rubber was deafening.

'Woohoo!' the man shouted with an excited nod when TJ had finished. His voice echoed through the trees.

I took out my phone, made sure that the flash was off, and started taking photographs. I got close ups of TJ, the man's face, and the gun itself.

TJ handed the gun to the man who then took a few steps forward and shot a few more bursts into the tyres.

Then he turned and hi-fived TJ before handing the gun back to him.

Drug dealing and now selling firearms, eh? I thought to myself. *TJ is really going up in the world.*

I was shocked, although I'd always known TJ was moronic, but there was part of me that was pleased. If I could somehow manufacture his arrest for the possession and sale of prohibited firearms, then he could face up to 10 years in prison. <u>And</u> given the fact that he was already on bail for a violent offence, he would definitely be placed on remand.

However, it did also give me a darker thought. If he had access to automatic weapons, how was I going to protect Caitlin and Sam if he decided to come to the farmhouse?

I signalled to Annie that it was time to return to the truck.

It was darker now than when we'd first arrived, and I had to strain my eyes to see the path that we'd taken through the trees. I could just about see the Ford Ranger which was parked about forty yards away.

Placing my foot down, I felt a wooden branch beneath my boot.

It snapped loudly.

Shit!

I froze.

The sound seemed to echo around the whole forest.

Bollocks!

I glanced back, and could tell that TJ and the man had also heard it.

In her panic, Annie brushed against some undergrowth and it shook, giving our location away.

'Oi!' TJ yelled angrily.

I grabbed hold of Annie's jacket and pulled her with me. 'Run,' I said under my breath.

CRACK! CRACK! CRACK!

The air exploded with the noise of the machine gun.

I heard a bullet whizz past my ear.

Shit! This is not good.

Keeping as low as I could, I kept hold of Annie's jacket as we weaved our way through the trees.

'Oi!' TJ yelled again.

I could hear that he and the man were now making their way through the trees and chasing us.

I wasn't going to look back. And we had a decent head start.

CRACK! CRACK!

A bullet hammered into a tree trunk about five yards to my left.

That was way too close.

'Frank!' Annie said quietly. She sounded scared.

'It's okay,' I reassured her. 'We can't stop and we need to keep low.'

CRACK!

A few seconds later, we got to the pick-up.

I opened the passenger door, making sure that Annie was getting in safely before running around to the driver's door.

I pushed the ignition and stamped down on the accelerator.

CRASH!

The back window of the Ranger's cab dissolved in a shower of glass as a bullet hit it.

'Oh my God!' Annie squealed and put her hands over her head.

I switched on the headlights and swerved right and then left, trying to make us a moving target and therefore harder to hit.

CRACK! CRACK!

I veered right and pulled the handbrake to make a sharp perpendicular turn on the muddy surface.

We reached the track that led down to the main road.

Spinning the steering wheel to the right, I floored the accelerator.

The Ranger lurched forward as we accelerated away.

Annie held on to her seat for dear life.

Hitting the bumps and muddy potholes at high speed, we were thrown and bounced around the inside of the cab.

I didn't care as long as it meant that we got away safely.

When we reached the main road I turned left.

It was a relief to get onto the smooth surface of a road. We sped away back towards Dolgellau.

'You okay?' I asked anxiously as we hammered around the bend.

'Never better,' Annie said dryly as she picked pieces of glass from her hair. 'Although a blanket and a cosy crime drama might be the better choice next time.'

Chapter 16

I parked my truck at the farmhouse in darkness, and glanced down at my phone to check again if the tracker that I'd put on TJ's car was working. The GPS showed that the tracker, and therefore TJ's car, were now at his home address.

Giving the Ford Ranger a quick check, I could see that by some miracle the only damage was to the back glass of the cab. More importantly, Annie and I had managed to get out of there without a scrape.

I took a moment as I gazed down at the paddock. Caitlin was walking Duke back towards the stables. Sam was beside her with Lleuad in tow. After my encounter with TJ, my gritty determination to keep them both safe felt even more resolute. The fact that he had access to automatic weapons made me very concerned and anxious. I'd have to beef up the security at the annexe and farmhouse.

I wandered down towards the paddock. A huge moon sat easily on the shoulders of the nearby mountains. I'd heard on the radio it was a 'blood moon'. According to Welsh folklore, a blood moon represented the dark, ominous side of the Welsh goddess Cerridwen. She was the keeper of *The Cauldron of Knowledge*. Cerridwen and her husband Tagad Foel had a very deformed son, Afagddu, and a beautiful daughter, Creirwy. The legend tells how Cerridwen brewed up a potion from her magic cauldron to give to her son to make him beautiful. However, Creirwy sabotaged this as she didn't want her brother to be as beautiful as herself. Taking the potion herself, Creirwy thought that it would make her even more beautiful but it had the opposite effect. Now disfigured and hideous, Creirwy saw her shocking reflection in a lake in Eryri/Snowdonia and was so distraught that she walked into the lake and drowned herself. It was another cheery legend from the canon of Welsh folktales.

Somewhere, a long way off, an owl hooted rhythmically and broke my train of thought. Jack must have sensed my presence, as he came bounding up the track from the paddock and jumped up at me.

'Hello boy,' I said, stroking and scruffing the top of his head. I loved the very bones of him. He was so loyal and protective. As far as I was concerned, he was as important as everyone else in my family.

'Taid!' Sam shouted as he gave me a wave.

'Hello mate. You been riding?' I asked as I approached.

'Yes. Just round the paddock.'

I gestured to the stables. 'Go and get Lleuad settled for the night, would you? I need to talk to your mum.'

Sam nodded but he looked a little wary as he walked away.

Caitlin gave me a quizzical look. 'Everything okay?'

'I found TJ,' I said under my breath.

'Where is he?'

'Tal-y-llyn.'

She looked concerned. It wasn't more than ten miles away.

'Right.' She nodded, trying to assess what I'd just told her. 'I was hoping that he was long gone, but I guess that was just wishful thinking.'

'Yeah. I'm afraid it was. I followed him earlier. Looks like he's got himself involved in selling firearms.'

I'd decided it wasn't a good idea to show her the photos of TJ selling or firing machine guns. She was worried enough already.

Her eyes widened. 'What? How the hell did that happen?'

I shrugged. 'No idea, but he has access to some serious firepower. And that makes me very nervous.'

Caitlin took a visible breath. 'Maybe me and Sam should go and live somewhere else where he can't find us.'

'No. No way.' I shook my head adamantly. 'You're safer here where I can protect you. I've put a tracker on his car so I can see where he is.'

'I can't believe I've brought all this to your and Mum's doorstep.' Caitlin looked a bit teary. 'I'm so sorry, Dad.'

'Hey,' I whispered, and gave her a hug. 'You're not responsible for what that scumbag decides to do with his life.'

Caitlin looked full of guilt and regret. 'I know, but this is the man I decided to have a child with.'

I sighed. 'Hey, we all make mistakes. Anyway, I've got something for you.'

'Sounds ominous.'

'It's a shotgun.'

Caitlin looked nervous. 'I haven't fired a shotgun since I was a teenager, and even then I wasn't a very good shot.'

'Well, in the morning I'm going to teach you how to

be. And I think you were better than you remember. I'm not always going to be here, and you need to be able to protect yourself, Sam, and your mother if you ever need to.'

Chapter 17

I walked through our farmhouse into the kitchen, grabbed a can of bitter, and poured it into a glass. I watched the frothy head slowly disappear. Rachel wasn't sitting in her chair in the living room so I assumed that she'd gone to bed. I sat down, took a long swig of bitter, and then blew out my cheeks. Memories of being shot at, the glass in the truck exploding, and our narrow escape were still at the forefront of my mind. Despite her reassurances, I felt guilty at having put Annie in so much danger. She'd had enough to deal with in the past few months.

Hearing a faint creak of a floorboard above, I realised that Rachel wasn't in bed. She had gone to sit in James' bedroom. In the ten years since his death, Rachel and I had almost never ventured in there. It was too painful. But in recent months, Rachel had spent increasing amounts of time sitting on his bed and looking through his stuff. I imagined that it had something to do with her diagnosis of Lewes body dementia – LBD. Rachel's most lucid moments were when she recalled the past. Her short-term memory seemed to be getting worse and worse with every week that passed. It was heartbreaking to see her get upset or frustrated when she struggled to recall the simplest of things.

Getting to my feet, I gave the little groan that seemed to be part and parcel of getting old and doing anything that required any exertion. I wandered out of the kitchen, down the hallway, and up the stairs.

I walked along the landing and stopped at James' door. There was a Wrexham FC sticker, an Acid House smiley face, and a blue logo for the band *Oasis*. Another sign read *James' Room – KEEP OUT!* I smiled at the memory of him trying to explain to me what exactly *Acid House* music was. I was as baffled then as I am now.

I gave a gentle knock and then opened the door slowly.

Rachel was sitting propped up on James' bed looking at a red Wrexham Football Club programme.

'Hello love,' I said with a kind smile as I went over and gave her a kiss.

'He was a mascot, wasn't he?' she asked, holding up the football programme.

I nodded and sat on the edge of the bed beside her. 'That's right.' I peered at the programme. *1st March 1988 Wrexham v Cambridge United.*

'How old was he then?' she asked.

'Seven,' I replied. 'We took him down to the old club shop to get his kit the day before.'

For a moment, I could remember the excitement on James' face as he got dressed in the replica kit, and my pride as he walked out with the team onto the pitch at The Racecourse Ground. I got a lump in my throat.

'That's right,' Rachel said with a smile. 'He insisted on getting the shirt with short sleeves. And I thought he was going to catch his death of cold wearing it. But he didn't.'

'No, he didn't,' I said quietly.

She put the programme down and then looked at me. 'Do you think we failed him as parents, Frank?'

I was taken aback for a moment. It was the most lucid thing Rachel had said in weeks.

I looked in her eyes and saw the life was back. The intelligence and wisdom that I'd fallen in love with all those years ago.

'I don't know,' I sighed. 'I just don't know. But it was my job as his father to protect him and I couldn't do that.'

'It was both of our jobs. Why was he so incredibly sad and lost?'

'I wish I knew,' I admitted, feeling the guilt and pain deep in my gut. 'I think about it every day.'

Rachel then looked confused. 'What about a headstone, Frank?' She sounded a little agitated and I could see that the clarity of mind had left her. 'We need to get him a headstone, don't we?'

'We got him a headstone, love,' I reassured her.

'Did we?'

'Yes.'

'Is it a nice headstone?'

I nodded, but I felt a sudden pang of guilt at her question. Even though Rachel and I had picked the headstone together, I'd never visited James' grave. I couldn't bring myself to go. I didn't know if that was selfish, but the longer I had put it off, the harder it had become in my head.

'Yes, it's a beautiful headstone.'

'Maybe we could go and see it, Frank?' She sat up and leaned over to the long black CD player.

'Yes, we should,' I agreed, but I knew that she'd forget this conversation in seconds.

She sifted through James' CDs. Then she selected one and pressed play.

'Come and sit here, you daft bugger,' she said with a smile as she patted the bed next to her.

Slide Away by *Oasis* started to play. It wasn't my kind of music but that didn't matter. It was one of James' favourite songs and we'd played it at his funeral.

Taking a deep breath to stop myself from crying, I moved closer to her.

She put her head on my chest as we listened to the music. The lyrics seemed so incredibly poignant.

Chapter 18

'Here you go,' said Sian Daniels, Marcus' wife, as she put mugs of coffee down in front of me and Annie.

We'd arrived at the house about ten minutes earlier. I made the excuse that I just wanted to check on how she was doing. Even though that was true, I also wanted to flag up my suspicions about Marcus' death with her. If anyone knew how he was feeling, or if there was anything worrying him in the days leading up to his death, it would be Sian. I just wasn't sure how she was going to react to me telling her my suspicions. Plus, I had the information that Richard Daniels had given us yesterday about his son and the state of his marriage. It didn't sound like it was always a harmonious one.

Annie started the conversation. 'I remember Marcus from when I was part of the legal team that looked into the veterans' compensation claim against the MOD.'

'Bastards,' Sian hissed angrily. 'It was a bloody cover up.'

Annie nodded sympathetically. 'I was certain that we had a very strong case, and Marcus was so passionate about getting justice for his fellow soldiers. He was such a good spokesman for them all.'

'That's why he was so upset when the case collapsed.' Sian shook her head. 'He never really got over it, and his health suffered over the years. I'm pretty sure that's a big reason why he did what he did.'

I took a moment and then decided to take the plunge. 'You know I'm not entirely convinced that Marcus did take his own life, Sian.'

The colour visibly drained from her face. 'What?' she gasped. 'I don't understand. What do you mean?'

'There are a couple of things that didn't add up when I saw him,' I tried to explain very gently. 'The position of the stepladder was all wrong. Mud on the steps but not his slippers.'

'We've spoken to the Chief Pathologist,' Annie added. 'There is a possibility that Marcus was injected with something before he died.'

'What? Injected? I don't understand.' Sian shook her head as her eyes widened in shock. 'You're saying that you think someone did this to Marcus?'

I nodded. 'I'm afraid so.'

'No, that's not right,' she said adamantly, shaking her head. 'The police were here for hours. Why are you saying all this?'

'We just thought we owed it to you to tell you our concerns.' I got the sense that she was not only thrown, but annoyed.

She put her hand to her face in disbelief. 'The police would have told me if there was anything suspicious.'

A man in his early 50s came through the doorway. He was thick-set, wearing a red plaid shirt, and had a wiry greying beard.

He looked concerned as he approached. 'What's going on, Sian?'

Sian looked up at him with a distraught expression. 'These people think that Marcus was ....'

Then she stopped. She didn't seem to be able to say it.

'What?' he prompted her.

'They think someone might have killed him,' she virtually whispered.

'What?' He pulled a perplexed face and glanced at me and Annie. 'And who the hell are you?' he asked angrily before looking back at Sian. 'Who are they?'

'It's all right, Owen,' she sighed, clearly trying to diffuse his anger. 'This is Frank, and his friend, Annie. Frank was riding past on Sunday morning when I found Marcus. He helped me, and he was a detective for a very long time.'

Owen gave me the once-over and looked at me suspiciously. 'But not anymore, eh?'

I nodded and said quietly, 'No, not anymore.'

'I don't like to see my sister upset,' he said confrontationally. 'Why the hell would you think that someone had killed Marcus?'

'Just a few things that didn't add up when I saw him on Sunday,' I replied.

'Yeah, well I think we'll let the police get on with their job. If they think that he took his own life, that's good enough for me and Sian,' he stated forcefully. Then he gave Sian a scornful look. 'I don't know why you're listening to any of these far-fetched theories, Sian.'

I could see that we weren't going to get any further now that Sian's brother had come into the equation, but Sian had information that we couldn't get anywhere else.

'There are just a couple of things,' I said calmly. 'Apart from all the stuff that was going on at his school, had

Marcus fallen out or had any arguments with anyone recently?'

'No,' Owen snapped immediately.

Sian stared at him defiantly. 'Come on, Owen. That's not true, is it?'

He paused for a moment. 'Oh, you mean your bloody sister-in-law?'

She nodded, as if he was being stupid. 'Of course.'

'You can't get her involved in this,' Owen remonstrated.

'If I'm honest, I don't care,' Sian said sharply before looking at me. 'Glynis was a bitch to my brother. She was his sister but she was only out for herself. They had a massive row here on New Year's Eve morning.'

I exchanged a glance with Annie. Was that significant?

'Do you know what they were arguing about?' Annie asked.

'The usual. Their dad, Richard.'

'I know Richard,' I said. 'He's a very old friend of mine. In fact, I went to see him yesterday to give him my condolences.'

'Oh right.' Sian said. 'Well, you might know then that Marcus was always there visiting him, or taking him stuff if he needed it. His Parkinson's is pretty bad now.'

'Yeah, and the only time Glynis ever went to see him is if she wanted to wheedle some money out of poor old Richard,' Owen added.

'Maybe we could go and talk to her?' I suggested. I'd seen more than my fair share of family squabbles over money and inheritance deteriorate into violence and worse.

'Good luck,' Owen snorted, and then turned and walked out of the room.

'You'll have to excuse my brother,' Sian said apologetically. 'He's very protective of me.'

'Of course he is,' Annie reassured her, 'and so he should be.'

'Do you think you could give us Glynis' address?' I asked.

'Yes, that shouldn't be a problem.' She pulled out her phone. 'She'll probably tell you to piss off. That's just what she's like.'

She turned the phone towards me and I used my own phone to take a photograph of the local address that was on the screen.

I noticed that the expression on Sian's face had changed, as if she had suddenly thought of something. 'Actually …' She paused and shook her head. 'Sorry, it's nothing,' she mumbled as she put her phone down on the kitchen table.

'Go on,' I encouraged her. 'Whatever it is, however small, it might be useful.'

'You said something about Marcus being injected, didn't you?'

Annie nodded. 'That's right.'

Then she gave us both a curious look. 'Funny thing is, his sister Glynis is a beautician. She's got her own company. She spends half her life injecting people with Botox, fillers, and all that.'

I shot Annie a look. Was that significant?

Chapter 19

Annie and I walked along the pathway to the cottage next door to the Daniel's home. I knew that police officers would have taken some form of statement from them on Sunday morning. However, given that the police weren't treating Marcus' death as suspicious, this statement would have been basic and routine. I wondered if they'd seen anything on New Year's Eve that might give us a clue as to what had happened. The neighbours might also have seen something going on at the Daniel's home that Sian hadn't told us about. I was often amazed when investigating a major crime, especially in rural areas like this, about how much information neighbours knew about one another - the comings, the goings, arguments. I assumed it was the exact opposite of a major city where people barely knew their neighbours.

Knocking at the door, I took a step back. There were cracks and weeds in the path. The paintwork needed a new lick of paint, and the wooden window frames on the ground floor were rotten. Taking a few more steps back, I saw that there were no lights on in the house despite it being a grey, dismal day. And there were no cars on the driveway.

'Looks like they're out,' Annie said after about a minute.

I nodded, and then clocked that they had a very new-looking video doorbell.

'Interesting,' I said as I pointed to it.

'Looks like it might cover some of the approaching road,' Annie stated.

I took a piece of paper from my notepad, scribbled my name and mobile number, and then posted it through the door.

We turned and walked back towards where I'd parked at the Daniels' home. Over in the corner, I spotted the same dark green Land Rover Defender that had been parked there every time I'd been to the cottage. Then I looked over to the other side of the gravel parking area. There was a silver VW Golf and a black Audi A3.

'Something up?' Annie asked me.

'Three cars.'

She shrugged. 'I'm not with you.'

'If I was to guess, I'd say that the Golf and the Audi belong to Sian and Marcus. I'd be surprised if they also have an old Land Rover. So, my assumption is that it belongs to Sian's brother, Owen.'

'Okay. And that's interesting because?'

'I'm not sure yet, but I'm 99% certain that it has been parked there ever since I rode past here with Sam on News Year's Day morning. Which means that Owen was in the house when Sian discovered Marcus' body.'

Annie frowned. 'Except you never saw him that day.'

'Precisely. Sian discovered that her husband had hanged himself the night before in a disused feed store in the garden. Why didn't she go and tell her brother immediately if he was here? Instead, she sat with me and then spoke to the police. In fact, there's never been any mention that Owen was here that night. Doesn't that strike you as strange?'

Annie nodded in agreement. 'Of course, but we don't know that he was here.'

'Probably worth us finding out,' I said under my breath.

I used my phone's camera to take a quick photo of the Land Rover and its registration number just in case I needed to do some more digging.

We turned and walked over the gravel towards my new pick-up. I'd used some plywood to make a temporary shield at the back of the cab where the bullet had shattered the glass.

'Are we ruling out O'Dowd and Morris entirely now?' Annie asked as she got into the passenger seat.

'I don't think we can. At least not Kevin O'Dowd,' I replied as I fastened my seatbelt.

I'd brought Jack with us. He nuzzled into me as I stroked his head and scruffed under his chin. His tongue lolled a little out of his mouth.

'No alibi, and a very strong motive for killing Marcus,' I continued, 'but my instinct is still that the injecting and making his death appear as a suicide is far too sophisticated and subtle.'

'I agree,' Annie said. 'Let's see what this Glynis Daniels has to say.'

I reached over Jack and opened my glove compartment. I rummaged around and pulled out a small leather wallet.

'What's that?' Annie asked as she stroked Jack's head.

'I get the feeling that Glynis Daniels isn't going to talk to us just because we have suspicions about her brother's death.' I opened the wallet and showed Annie my old private investigator's licence. 'When I left the North Wales Police, I did some work for a couple of years as a private investigator. Mainly insurance fraud and suspicious husbands and wives.'

'Frank, this licence expired in 2015!'

I shrugged. 'Maybe she won't check it.'

She shook her head and rolled her eyes.

Chapter 20

Fifteen minutes later we pulled into Corris, a small village on the southern Eryri/Snowdonia and Powys border. It had been built to house the miners who worked in the nearby slate mines.

Parking outside a nice-looking detached house, Annie and I got out of the truck and made our way up to the front door. There was a brand new white BMW and a black Land Rover Discovery on the driveway. It looked as if Glynis, and whoever she lived with, had a very comfortable life.

From somewhere inside came a ferocious barking. Whatever dog was inside, it scratched furiously at the door as I rang the doorbell.

A few seconds later, the front door opened.

A woman in her late 40s, lots of make-up, false eyelashes, and a spray tan, held a Staffordshire Bull Terrier back by his collar. She was wearing a bright blue velour tracksuit.

'Yes?' she asked, looking thoroughly annoyed that I'd rung the doorbell.

'We're looking for Glynis?' I said over the noise of the barking.

She winced as if she couldn't hear me over the din. Then she pulled the dog roughly and put him into a nearby room.

'Sorry. I couldn't hear what you were asking,' she said as she came back to the door. 'If this is some kind of charity thing, I'm not interested. I donate online.'

'No, no,' I reassured her as I took out my licence. 'We're private investigators. We're looking into your brother's death. I'm so sorry for your loss.'

'We know this must be a difficult time for you,' Annie added.

If I was honest, there was nothing about Glynis' manner or appearance that would suggest her brother had taken his own life only two days' earlier.

'Private investigators?' she asked with a slight sneer. 'I don't understand. Who are you working for?'

'I'm afraid I can't break our client's anonymity,' I explained calmly, 'but we do believe that your brother died in suspicious circumstances.'

'Eh?' She looked baffled. 'Marcus hanged himself in that old feed shed. What suspicious circumstances?'

If Glynis was upset or grieving for her brother, she was doing a hell of a good job of hiding it.

Annie gestured inside. 'If you can spare a few minutes, could we come in and explain?'

'No, it's all right thanks. It all sounds very odd to me,' she said, shaking her head with an unfriendly smirk, 'and I've got lots to get on with. I've got to go and try to explain to our father what my selfish bastard of a brother has done.'

As she began to close the door, I had a thought.

'I understand that you were arguing with Marcus about

your father the afternoon before he died,' I announced, hoping that this might prevent her from shutting the door in our faces.

It did.

She fixed me with an inquisitive stare. 'You've been talking to Sian?'

'Yes.'

She thought for a moment and then opened the door wider. 'You'd better come in. I meant what I said though, I haven't got much time.'

ANNIE and I were sitting in the modern, rather tasteless, living room. Everything was grey or white. There were throws, blankets, and big cushions everywhere. On one wall was a huge black and white portrait photograph of Glynis and a tough-looking man with a shaved head in his 40s whom I assumed was her husband. It was one of those cheesy glossy photos from a photographer's studio.

On the wall to our right was an enormous flatscreen television that looked to me as if it had been taken from a cinema. For a second, I thought back to the tiny black and white television that Rachel and I had rented from a local shop when we first got married. I'd completely forgotten that until the 1990s, no one had enough money to buy their own televisions. So, they rented them.

Glynis sat forward and stared at us. I'd already gone through our suspicions about Marcus' death – the steps, the mud, and possible injection mark. I was trying to suss out whether she was involved in her brother's death, but she wasn't really giving anything away. She wasn't showing much emotion at his death but, in my experience, someone who was guilty would usually try to fake emotion to hide their guilt. And she definitely wasn't doing that.

Annie leaned forward. 'Going back to what Frank mentioned earlier, Sian said that you might have been arguing about your father? Is that right?'

'Not that it's any of your business,' she said defensively, 'but yes, we did have an argument. I don't want anyone thinking that I'm hiding anything. Or pointing any bloody fingers in my direction. I didn't always see eye to eye with my brother, but I still loved him.'

'Of course,' I said empathetically, but I wasn't convinced. 'We're just trying to get a clear picture of his state of mind on the day leading up to his death.' I scratched at my beard. 'Can you tell us what you were arguing about?'

Glynis took a deep breath and gave an audible sigh. 'My father gave me some money when I was setting up my beauty business about ten years ago. It was meant to be between me and him. Somehow Marcus found out and went mental. And then when I grew that business into a success, he couldn't seem to be happy for me. I knew that he still resented the fact that our father had given me the money. Sometimes he would drink too much and it would all come out. All that poison. According to him, the only reason I had such a comfortable lifestyle was because of that money our father gave me.' Glynis sneered. 'Nothing to do with all the hours and hard work I'd put into the business for the last ten years.'

'Did Marcus ever confront your father about all this?' Annie asked.

'Not really. It was all bullshit anyway. Our father had offered him money when he'd had all the health problems after he came out of the army. Marcus turned him down. As far as I was concerned, that was his problem.'

'Can you tell us where you were between midnight and 1am on New Year's Day?' I asked.

'Are you taking the piss?' she said angrily. 'You think I killed Marcus?'

'I was just asking,' I said calmly, 'and, of course, you don't have to tell us.'

She gave an audible huff. 'David and I were in The Royal Oak in Ffestiniog. We stayed overnight at the pub.'

Chapter 21

Fifteen minutes later, Annie and I were making our way towards Bontnewydd. Not only did I feel obliged to check in with Richard again, I also wanted to double check what Glynis had told us about her relationship with her father and with Marcus. Plus I wanted to check out her alibi.

My phone buzzed and I grabbed it to check. It was a message.

Annie held out her hand. 'Would you like me to read it?'

'Erm, I'm fine,' I said.

She raised an eyebrow. 'Actually, I insist. That way you can keep your eyes on the road and we won't crash.'

I gave her a wry smile. 'Since you put it like that …' I handed her my phone. 'Password is 120852.'

'Which is the date of your birth.'

'You remembered?'

'No. But I know you were born in 1952.'

'Right. Well thanks Sherlock,' I quipped. 'Who's the message from?'

She tapped at my phone screen. 'DS Kelly Thomas. She wants to meet to talk about the police investigation into Marcus' death. Off the record. She's suggesting 3pm at Cymer Abbey?'

'Sounds good to me. Wonder what that's about?'

'Maybe the post-mortem?' Annie suggested.

'Maybe.'

She handed me back my phone. 'Here you go. I've said we'll be there.'

The temperature outside had dropped significantly, and snow had started to fall heavily all around us as we drove. It had started to settle, so the heathland and hills were dusted with an ever-increasing blanket of white.

Jack was now lying down in between us having a snooze.

Annie put her hand gently on his head. 'He's part of the family, isn't he?'

'He's my best friend.'

She looked offended. 'I thought I was your best friend?'

'Sort of,' I joked.

'Sort of.' She pushed my arm playfully.

'You're my best human friend,' I added, 'but me and Jack … it's just on a different level.'

She grinned. 'Oh, well that's charming!' Then she reached over to the car stereo and pressed a button.

'Bingo,' she said brightly.

I gave her a quizzical look.

She held up her phone. 'You've got Bluetooth in this car.'

'It's a truck,' I corrected her.

'Pedant,' she teased. 'And that means I can play some of my music for once.'

'Okay,' I said suspiciously.

She scrolled on her phone and then pressed play.

To my relief, *Fire and Rain* by *James Taylor* started to play.

'I love James Taylor,' I said with a smile. 'He's country. Just with a bit of folk.'

Annie rolled her eyes. 'Oh, well I'm glad it meets with your approval, sire,' she joked. 'You know that Taylor Swift is named after James Taylor? He was her parents' favourite singer.'

'Remind me who Taylor Swift is again.' I knew the name but I couldn't remember what she looked like, or any of her songs.

'Sometimes I think you live under a rock, Frank,' Annie groaned. Then she looked down at her phone. 'Okay, here we go.'

Fearless by *Taylor Swift* started to play.

Even though I didn't recognise the song, it was clear that it was country music.

'This is Taylor Swift?'

Annie laughed. 'Yes.'

'Oh, well I like this,' I admitted.

We drove for the next few minutes listening to the music as the snow fell onto the windscreen.

Eventually, we pulled up outside Richard's home.

I parked and we got out. Jack was still fast asleep.

The snow was getting thicker on the ground, and it crunched under my boots as we walked quickly up the garden path to the front door.

I knocked, and a few seconds later it was opened by Richard.

'Come in, come in,' he said, beckoning us inside. His hands and arms were shaking.

'Sorry to trouble you again, Richard,' I said as I shook the snow from my coat.

'Not at all. Not at all. Come through.'

He led us through to the living room where we'd been the day before. His walking and shaking seemed a lot worse than during our previous visit.

'I'd offer to make you guys a coffee, but as you can see the stress of Marcus' death has made my condition much worse. I'd probably spill most of the bloody coffee before it even got to you.'

'I'm sorry to hear that.' I gave him an empathetic look.

'I had a detective here earlier,' he said. 'A young woman. Kelly?'

I nodded. 'DS Kelly Thomas.'

'That's right.' Richard looked confused. 'She seemed to think that something had come up in Marcus' post-mortem that needed to be checked?'

'We've spoken to the Chief Pathologist,' I said calmly. 'He's a very old friend of mine.' Then I stopped for a second. I wasn't quite sure how to broach the subject of the injection.

Richard clearly sensed my hesitation. 'Please, Frank. Whatever it is, I'd prefer to know.'

'He thought that Marcus might have been injected with something before he died,' I said gently. 'Possibly a strong sedative or an anaesthetic.'

'Oh God …' he whispered as he blinked and then took a handkerchief to dab his eyes. I could see the pain and grief on his face. It made me more determined to find out exactly what had happened to Marcus. I owed it to Richard to give him some peace of mind and closure.

He sniffed and gave me a forced smile. 'Sorry, I just don't understand why someone would want to do something like that to Marcus.' His gaze flicked between us. 'Unless you two think it has something to do with that girl at his school?'

'We don't think it does,' Annie said quietly.

'We've met the father and the boyfriend,' I added. 'To put it politely, I think they lack the intelligence to stage something like this. And the boyfriend has an alibi.'

'I see.' Richard sighed and then shook his head. 'As a father, it's just so devastating to think that there was someone out there who wanted to kill my son. Do you have any idea who might have done this?'

'I'm sorry,' I replied. 'We're not sure at the moment, but we've been trying to get a full a picture of Marcus' life in the days leading up to his death.'

'Of course.'

I sat forward on the sofa. 'We went to speak to your daughter, Glynis.'

'Glynis?' Richard narrowed his eyes. 'You don't think she had something to do with …' Then his voice tailed off.

'No, no,' I reassured him, although at this stage I wasn't prepared to rule anyone out. And Glynis was clearly hiding something when she spoke to us. 'It's just that Sian had mentioned that Marcus and Glynis had had a blazing row in the afternoon of New Year's Eve. I just wanted to ask her what it was about, that's all.'

His lips creased in a grimace. 'It would have been about money, I'm afraid. And unfortunately, I'm partially to blame for all that.'

'How do you mean?' Annie asked.

'I loaned Glynis a substantial amount of money about a decade ago. She wanted to start up a beauty business. She needed to get the required training, buy the equipment. It wasn't cheap but she's done very well for herself.'

I scratched my beard. 'You said that you *loaned* her the money?'

'Yes, and unfortunately I've been unable to persuade

her to pay it back. I have a decent teacher's pension but I'm not a wealthy man.'

'And this was a source of conflict between Glynis and Marcus?'

'Yes. Continually. And Glynis had asked to borrow more money recently. When Marcus found that out, he went ballistic.'

I glanced at Annie for a moment. I wondered if this argument and resentment had anything to do with Marcus' death. If anything, it had been Marcus who was furious with his sister.

Annie gave Richard a sympathetic look. 'Were Marcus and Glynis your only two children?'

'Yes.'

'That must have made things very difficult.'

'I'm afraid it did,' Richard admitted, 'but I did reassure Marcus that I'd recently put stuff in place that would redress the balance when I was gone.'

I gave him a questioning look. I assumed that he meant something legal. Before I could quiz him any further, there was a knock at the door.

Richard glanced down at his watch and then started to get up from his chair. 'Oh, right. Sorry, I'd completely forgotten that I have a physio arriving. I didn't even think to cancel.'

'We'll leave you to it,' Annie said as we got up.

As we went towards the door, Richard looked at me. 'I can't tell you how much I appreciate what you and Annie are doing.'

'Not a problem,' I said as we went out into the hallway. 'We just want to get justice for Marcus.'

As we moved towards the front door, I spotted a letter sitting on the small table under a mirror. It had *Martin Jones*

& Sons Solicitors written at the top. In bold writing it had **Richard Daniels – *Last Will and Testament***.

Before I could read any more, Richard had opened the front door to allow the physio in and for us to leave.

My guess was that he had recently made changes to his will.

Chapter 22

'Here you go,' Martin Jones said as he put down two mugs of coffee and a plate of biscuits in front of me and Annie. We were sitting at a large meeting table in *Martin Jones & Sons* solicitors in Dolgellau.

Martin was balding, with glasses and a podgy nose.

I'd been using the firm for the past thirty years, and Martin's late father, Arthur, who established the firm in the 1960s, had been my solicitor.

The room was old fashioned, with dark green walls, oak furniture, and shelves stacked with box files and folders. It smelled like an old library. I spotted a photograph of Arthur and Martin standing on the high street in front of the office. It must have been the late 70s as Martin was only a boy and, at a guess, he must now be in his 50s.

'Your dad was a good man,' I said, gesturing to the photo.

'Yeah, he was,' Martin agreed. 'I never got to thank you for doing the reading at his funeral.'

'It was an honour.' By my calculations, the funeral had been about five years ago and I hadn't seen Martin since, except for the odd wave in the pub or on the high street. I was aware that given Rachel's illness, I needed to amend my will and give power of attorney to Caitlin in case anything happened to me. But that was for another day.

'I've just come from Richard Daniel's place,' I said to Martin as he pulled his seat forward.

He shook his head sadly. 'I couldn't believe the news. I was at school with Marcus.' Then his expression changed as he looked at me. 'And James of course.'

'That's right.'

'So sad,' he said quietly. 'Both Marcus and James.'

He was referring to the fact that as far as he knew both Marcus and my son James had taken their own lives.

'My friend Annie and I are helping Richard with a few things,' I said, wondering how I was going to broach the subject of Richard's will.

'Well, if there's anything I can do to help, just let me know,' he said earnestly.

'He mentioned that you've just done some legal work for him,' I said in as nonchalant a tone as I could muster.

Martin frowned. 'Did he?'

'Yes. He told me that you'd changed his will for him.' It was only a guess but it had to be worth a try.

He looked at me suspiciously. 'He told you that?'

'Yes. You remember my wife, Rachel?'

'Of course.'

'Unfortunately, she has a form of dementia,' I explained quietly.

'I'm so sorry to hear that.'

'I'd told Richard that I was going to have to talk to you guys about changing my will. I need your advice, but I assume that I should give my daughter, Caitlin, power of attorney over my estate in case something happens to me, as Rachel no longer has mental capacity.'

'Yes, we'd have to create an LPA for Caitlin,' he agreed. 'Obviously she'd need to come in with you.'

'Obviously.'

Annie gave me a curious glance, wondering what I was up to.

'Anyway, Richard told me that he'd made some significant amendments to his will. He told us you'd talked it through with him, but he said he'd have to come in again as he'd made Marcus the sole beneficiary of his will very recently, and that would need to change after what's happened.'

'Yes, that's right,' Martin said, sipping at his coffee thoughtfully. 'That had only just occurred to me as you said it. But Richard hadn't signed off on the will yet anyway.'

Moving my chair back, I gave him a half smile. 'Well, we won't take up any more of your time today. And I'm sure Richard will be in touch. I'll make an appointment to come in with Caitlin too.'

He got up and nodded. 'Absolutely. Good to see you, Frank.'

Chapter 23

'You're a sneaky bugger, Frank Marshal,' Annie said, giving me a knowing look.

We were driving to Cymer Abbey to meet DS Kelly Thomas.

'I'll take that as a compliment,' I laughed.

'Do we think Glynis is involved in Marcus' death?' she asked.

'Possibly. There's definitely motive. If she knew that Richard had changed the will and that everything was going to Marcus, then maybe she killed him to stop that happening. I don't expect that Richard is going to live for many more years.'

'No ... Maybe Marcus told her that afternoon and that's why they had such a massive row,' Annie suggested. 'Glynis goes home and broods on it. She decides to go back, murder her brother, and make it look like a suicide. She has access to syringes.'

'One problem.'

'I know ... she needed help.'

'Yeah, exactly,' I replied, 'but she's married. Maybe she

told her husband David what had happened and he agreed to help her?'

'Maybe, but we have no evidence. It feels like a bit of a stretch at the moment.'

'I agree. But it's all we've got.'

I glanced out and saw the dark brown sign marked *Cymer Abbey*.

We parked in the visitors' car park, got out, and looked around. It had stopped snowing about half an hour earlier but the snow was about three to four inches deep. There were only two other cars in the car park.

Annie groaned as her breath froze in clouds. 'All very clandestine, isn't it? Meeting at the ruins of an old abbey.'

We crunched through the snow and towards the old ruins. 'I don't suppose Kelly wants to be seen with me in case it gets back to Dewi.'

I was glad to be outside as it gave Jack a chance to have a run around and stretch his legs.

The original abbey had been built for Cistercian monks back in the 12th century.

'Of course, this place is haunted,' I said as we reached the ruins.

Annie laughed. 'Of course it is. It's an old monastery. I'd be very disappointed if it wasn't and there weren't the ghosts of old monks lurking around somewhere.'

'Cynic,' I joked. 'Every time I bring Jack here for a walk, the place completely freaks him out. His heckles go up. You watch him.'

He was bounding around in the snow without a care in the world.

I sighed. 'Yeah, well maybe not every time we come here.'

I spotted a figure out of the corner of my eye. It was

Kelly, and she was walking towards us from the middle of the stone ruins.

'It's still all very *The Third Man* and *Harry Lime*,' Annie said under her breath.

'Frank, Annie,' Kelly said as she got to us. She was wearing a thick, dark navy overcoat and a long, rust-coloured scarf that was wrapped several times around her neck and shoulders.

'Hi Kelly,' I said as I stamped my feet to try and get the feeling back in them.

'Sorry for all the cloak and dagger stuff,' she said apologetically. 'It's just that Dewi knows everyone everywhere. And I don't think he'd take too kindly to me meeting up with you.'

I nodded in agreement. 'No, I don't suppose he would, but that's because he's an egotistical prick who should be drummed out of the force.' I could feel myself getting angry just by discussing him.

'You've spoken to the Chief Pathologist?' Annie asked her, trying to move the conversation on.

'Yes. It's inconclusive, but Professor Fillery told me his theory that Marcus could have been injected with a powerful sedative. Given what you told us about what you discovered at the scene of Marcus' death, it all sounds very suspicious.'

'But not suspicious enough for you to launch a full investigation into his death, I presume?' I said.

'No.' Kelly gave a sigh. 'I'd like to take a closer look but …'

I tensed with annoyance. 'Let me guess. Dewi doesn't want to.'

'This isn't the first time this man has allowed personal prejudice to get in the way of a murder investigation,' Annie said a little sharply.

Kelly looked at her. Annie was referring to the ongoing IOPC investigation into North Wales Police's handling of a series of murders in 1997. There was a deep suspicion that Dewi had colluded with the senior investigating officer at the time – Ian Goddard – to find Keith Tatchell guilty of the murders. Tatchell had had an affair with Goddard's wife, but that was never taken into account at the time.

'I know,' Kelly said quietly. 'I'm doing my best to keep my side of the street clean.' Then she looked at me. 'And Frank, I've got the feeling that you're continuing to look into Marcus' death.'

'Yeah, I am,' I replied. 'His father, Richard Daniels, is an old friend. I owe it to him to find out exactly what happened to his son. That's the right thing to do.'

'I agree with you. If you need anything, let me know and I'll see what I can do.'

'Thank you,' I said. 'I need a couple of names for starters. Did you speak to Marcus' neighbour?'

'Mr Tinsdale? Yes. Bit of an oddball, but he just gave us a statement about Marcus and Sian. Nothing of great interest.'

'No, but as I'm sure you're more than aware Kelly, the problem is that Mr Tinsdale, and anyone else for that matter, wouldn't have been asked if they saw anything suspicious on New Year's Eve. Nor would they have been made aware that there were suspicious circumstances around Marcus' death. They would have been told that Marcus had taken his own life and nothing more than that. Which makes all those interviews and statements completely useless for our purposes.'

She moved a strand of hair from her face. 'Yes, unfortunately it does,' she admitted.

'Sian mentioned that an old army friend of Marcus'

had been to the house for lunch but then left late afternoon,' I said. 'Can you remember his name?'

Kelly took out her black police notebook and thumbed through it. 'Yes. Ollie Cannon. Address is Oakwood Cottage, Pen-y-Bryn, Harlech.'

Annie thanked Kelly and typed the information into her phone.

Kelly put her notebook away. 'What have you come up with so far?'

'Marcus had been accused of inappropriate behaviour towards Layla O'Dowd, a teenage girl at his school, and had been suspended from work.'

'Yes, his wife Sian told me that. She seemed to think it was a contributory factor in Marcus taking his own life.'

'We've had a word with Layla and her father Kevin O'Dowd, and we checked out Layla's boyfriend Adam Morris. O'Dowd and Morris are racist thugs with criminal records.'

Kelly narrowed her eyes. 'I sense there's a *but* coming?'

'Our instinct when we confronted O'Dowd was that he didn't know Marcus was dead. He claims he was in the flat above his pub at the time of the murder, but there's no one to verify that. He could be a very good actor but I'd be surprised. We also saw a time-stamped photo of Morris with Layla at his caravan on New Year's Eve, which gives him an alibi too. In any case, the MO is far too subtle and sophisticated for men like that. They want to take out their revenge with crude violence. Beat Marcus to death.

'Anyone else on your radar?' Kelly asked.

'There had been a nasty dispute between Marcus and his sister over their father's money and his estate,' I explained. 'Turns out that Richard asked his solicitor to draw up a new will a couple of weeks ago so that his daughter Glynis received next to nothing on the event of his death compared to Marcus.'

Kelly looked confused. 'Why?'

'Richard had lent her money which she'd never repaid,' Annie replied, 'and she'd asked for more recently. He wanted to make sure that Marcus got his fair share, but the will hasn't been signed yet.'

'AND YOU THINK Glynis might have killed Marcus because of that?'

'Strong motive,' I replied.

'Plus, Glynis is a trained beautician,' Annie added. 'She has access to syringes, and spends her life injecting people for a living.'

Kelly's eyes widened. 'She can't have done it on her own though.'

'No,' I agreed. 'We haven't spoken to her husband but she could have roped him in, especially if she was going to benefit financially from Marcus' death. As you probably noticed, Richard has Parkinson's. And that's life limiting.'

'Right, leave that with me. I'll do some digging around.'

Annie looked at her gratefully. 'Thank you.'

'Just one more thing,' I said, pulling out my phone. 'I've tracked down Caitlin's scumbag of a partner. Seems like he's graduated to a new type of business up here.' I went on to my camera roll and showed her the photos I'd taken of TJ and his customer firing a submachine gun into tyres in the forest.

Kelly looked horrified. 'Jesus, Frank! Where did you take this?'

'Forest at the foot of Cadair Idris. I can send it over with his address.'

'Yes please,' she said with a scandalised shake of her head.

I gave her a dark look. 'It would be good to get that scumbag locked up before he decides to pay me a visit, hurts my daughter, and takes my grandson. I've got a shotgun but it's no match for something like that.'

ANNIE and I made our way into The Royal Oak pub in Ffestiniog, a community of villages that dated back to the 13th century. The pub was modern and fashionable. It was all subtle shades of greens and greys, chalk boards, and micro-brewed beers.

I got to the bar and looked at Annie. 'Drink?'

'I'm all right, thanks. If I have something to drink I'll fall asleep in the truck on the way home. Especially if you start playing your music.'

'That's very rude,' I laughed, as I tried to attract the attention of the young barman in his 20s.

'Hi there,' he said as he came over. 'What can I get you?'

'Actually, I'm trying to track down a couple of friends of ours. Glynis and David Dixon. They said they stayed here on New Year's Eve.'

I took my phone and retrieved the photograph of Glynis that I'd taken from her Facebook profile page.

'This is Glynis,' I said as I turned the screen to him.

He looked blankly at the image. 'I don't remember her to be honest, but I was working at the other bar in our restaurant.' He gestured to a middle-aged woman with frizzy hair. 'I'll get Pat. She worked on New Year's Eve.'

I gave Annie a look. Had Glynis told us a barefaced lie about where she was on New Year's Eve?

A few seconds later, Pat came over with a friendly smile.

'You were asking about someone who stayed with us on New Year's Eve?' she asked. 'Is that right?'

'Yes.' I turned my phone screen to show her. 'Glynis Dixon.'

'Oh yes, I remember her.'

'She was here, was she?' Annie asked.

'That's right. With her husband, I think. I remember them because they bought two bottles of our most expensive champagne.'

'And they stayed overnight? Is that right?'

'Yes.'

'I don't suppose you remember what time they went up to their room?'

'They were down here at midnight,' she replied, starting to look a little suspicious at our questions. 'Why are you asking all this?'

I took out my expired private investigator's licence. 'I'm a private investigator.'

'Ooh!' Pat's face lit up. 'Were they having an affair?'

Annie ignored her question. 'Do you think they were here at 1am?'

She pulled a face. 'To be honest I'd had a few drinks by then so it's a bit of a blur, but I think they were.'

'You're not certain?' I asked to clarify.

'No, I couldn't swear to it, dear.'

'What about the morning?' Annie asked. 'Did you see them then?'

'Oh yes. A bit worse for wear,' she said with a nod. 'They came in here at eleven and had two large bloody marys.'

Chapter 24

'Okay,' I said gently. 'You just line up the can with the V at the end of the barrel.'

Caitlin nodded. 'Yeah, I remember.'

'Then take a long slow breath to steady yourself. Squeeze the trigger, don't pull at it.'

An hour earlier, I'd returned home and dug out my other shotgun that was in its case in the attic. I'd cleaned the barrels. Then I'd dismantled it, cleaned the firing mechanism and the chamber, and reassembled it. Even though it wasn't as new or powerful as my Winchester, it would still blow a hole the size of a bowling ball in a man at close range.

For the past twenty minutes, I'd been giving Caitlin a refresher course in how to shoot a shotgun. I'd taught both her and James how to shoot as teenagers, but I assumed that Caitlin was a little rusty.

I spotted Sam in my peripheral vision.

I put my hand up to stop him getting any closer. 'Just stay there, mate. No further.'

He looked at me and nodded.

'And put your fingers in your ears,' I added.

He immediately put his fingers into his ears and winced.

I tapped Caitlin on the shoulder. 'And away you go, Calamity Jane.'

BOOM!

The shotgun exploded with a thundering bang.

One of the large rusty oil cans that I'd positioned on the snow-covered dry stone wall flew back across the field and then landed in the snow.

'Great shot, Mum!' Sam yelled excitedly.

Caitlin grinned at us and blew on her knuckles. 'Still got it.'

'Can I have a go?' Sam asked.

'NO!' Caitlin and I replied in unison.

I looked at Sam's disappointed face. 'When you're a bit older, mate. These guns are very heavy.'

'And very dangerous,' Caitlin added, giving me a withering look as if to say *It's the dangerous bit that's important NOT the fact that they're heavy.*

Out of the corner of my eye, I saw Jack sniffing around the boundary wall about forty yards to our right. It was close to where our land ended and the farmland began. He circled, and then jumped up with his paws on the stone wall. He made a whimpering noise. Something wasn't right.

I looked at Caitlin. 'Give it another go?'

'Try and stop me,' she replied with a grin.

I signalled to Sam to put his fingers in his ears again.

Caitlin held the gun steady, closed one eye, and then squeezed the trigger.

BANG!

The second rusty petrol can flew away into the field.

'Looks like your mum's a born sharpshooter, Sam,' I laughed.

She looked at me. 'I guess I was taught well.'

I shrugged. 'Not much I can teach you anymore. You've got this.' I pointed to where Jack was sniffing around. 'Sam and I are going for a little wander up there.'

She frowned at me suspiciously. 'Everything all right?'

'Yeah, I'm sure it's nothing.' I put my hand on Sam's shoulder. 'Come on, mate.'

Our boots crunched on the snow as we walked up the path beside the wall. There was a stillness that came with a fall of snow. No noise from birds or animals. Just the soft thud of snow falling from a nearby overladen tree bough.

'Did you mean it, Taid?' Sam asked. 'Will you teach me to shoot when I'm older?'

'Yes, of course. But using a gun is a serious business, you know that? It's a huge responsibility.'

He nodded thoughtfully, but I wasn't sure that he knew exactly what I was trying to say. He was too young, but one day he'd understand what I meant.

We drew closer to Jack. Whatever it was, he'd picked up the scent of something.

'What's Jack doing?' Sam asked.

'I'm not sure yet. Maybe just the scent of an animal. He's definitely on to something.'

'Do you get wild animals in Snowdonia?' he asked.

'Not really. There have been sightings of big cats in the park though.'

He looked excited. 'Big cats? Like a leopard?'

I smiled. 'More like a puma or a lynx.'

'Oh, right.'

I wasn't going to tell him that two years ago I'd disturbed what I was pretty sure was a puma in the nearby woods. I didn't want to scare him. And I knew in reality that a puma was going to be far more scared of us than we were of it.

'What is it, boy?' I asked Jack as we reached the wall.

He came over to us and Sam gave him a stroke. 'What can you smell, boy?' he asked.

'Let's have a look, shall we?' I lifted Sam up onto the top of the flat surface of the stone wall, then climbed up and stood beside him.

At first, all I could see was the huge white carpet of virgin snow stretched out before us. The landscape was beautiful, and looked so completely different now that it was all pure white.

But then I spotted to our right that the perfect 'carpet' was broken by a small linear pattern that seemed to follow the wall's perimeter for as far as the eye could see.

It was the pattern of someone's footprints in the snow.

They stopped about ten yards from where we were standing, and then went back again.

Someone had walked down to the top end of our land on the other side of the wall. I wasn't sure why but it made me feel very uneasy.

Chapter 25

It was 8am when Annie and I parked outside the neighbour's home next to the Daniels' cottage. There had been no more snowfall overnight but it was still cold enough for it not to have thawed yet. We walked along the road and up the garden path. Glancing up, I could see that there was smoke coming from the chimney. Someone was in, and it smelled as if they were burning coal rather than wood.

As we'd driven past, I'd also noticed that there was now a blue Ford Escort van on the driveway. It had writing on it. A local plumbing firm.

I went to give the front door an authoritative knock before remembering the modern-looking video doorbell on the other side. I pressed it and heard it ring inside the cottage. Compared to the shabby state of the exterior, the doorbell, with its white light, seemed out of place.

With a quick look to my right, I saw the yellowing net curtains at a downstairs window twitch a little. Someone was checking us out before answering the door.

After about a minute, there was the sound of keys unlocking the front door and a safety chain being removed.

The door opened slowly and a man in his 60s peered out cautiously. He was completely bald, with a round face and beady dark eyes that peered at us through large oblong glasses that looked like they'd been bought in the 1980s. He wore a dark burgundy cardigan, ill-fitting grey trousers, and tartan slippers that had seen better days.

'Hello?' he asked, looking baffled and his eyes a little glazed. He was jittery, and moved behind the door as if this would somehow protect him.

'Hi there,' I said in a friendly tone. 'It's Mr Tinsdale isn't it?'

'That's right,' he answered nervously.

'We've been talking to your neighbour Sian next door,' I said, gesturing to her cottage. 'I'm sure you've heard about what happened to Marcus.'

'Yes, yes,' he replied, shaking his head. 'Horrible business. I only spoke to him on the afternoon before it happened.'

'New Year's Eve?' Annie asked.

'Aye, that's right.'

'It's just that we've agreed to help his family look into what happened that day,' I said, and then pointed to his doorbell. 'I noticed that you have one of these doorbells that records videos?'

'Yes, yes. Only had it a few months.' I could see that he wasn't up for letting us inside, despite the arctic temperature outside. 'Can't be too careful these days.'

'No ... Well, I'm a retired detective. We wondered if we could take a look at the video from it on New Year's Eve night? Around midnight?'

Tinsdale scratched nervously at his face and nose and

looked away for a few seconds. 'I don't see why you would want to do that.'

Bollocks. This isn't going to be as easy as I thought it was going to be.

'It'll only take a few minutes,' I said, trying to coax him along. 'We'd like to check who was coming and going that night. And your doorbell looks over the main road and the turning into the Daniels' driveway.'

He narrowed his eyes. 'I thought Marcus hanged himself?'

'We're not sure that he did,' Annie explained.

'Eh? What does that mean?' he asked.

'We're not sure what happened,' I admitted, and pointed to his doorbell again. 'But looking at the footage from this would help us.'

'That's something for the police to do, isn't it?' he said, and then peered closely at Annie. 'Don't I recognise you?'

She shrugged. 'I'm not sure.'

His face changed as he tried to remember where he recognised her from.

'Mold Crown Court?' she suggested. 'I worked for many years as a judge.'

The blood drained from Tinsdale's face as his eyes moved around. It was clear that he did recognise Annie from when she was a judge, and it had rattled him.

He shook his head adamantly. 'No, I don't think that's it.'

He's definitely lying.

He looked at both of us. 'If you want to see what's on my camera and laptop, you're going to have to come back with the police and a search warrant,' he snapped, and closed the door.

I shot a look at Annie. Tinsdale was definitely hiding something, and our visit had spooked him.

Chapter 26

'Yes, I've got it here,' Annie said as she looked down at her phone. She had been using her access to the Mold Court records to see if she could track down whether Tinsdale had appeared there. Without Ethan's help, we couldn't access his criminal record so it was one step at a time.

It had been fifteen minutes since we'd left Tinsdale's home, and we were now driving up to Harlech so we could speak to Ollie Canon, Marcus' old army friend who had been over at the cottage on New Year's Eve but, according to Sian, had left early afternoon.

Snowy hills and then mountains stretched up to our left and towered above us. The sky was now a luminous blue, with a few clouds that looked like stretched cotton wool.

'Go on,' I said, glancing over.

'Mr Robert Henry Tinsdale. 12th May 2007. Court number 1. Presiding Judge, me,' Annie said quietly. There was something about what she'd found that had made her feel uneasy.

'So, he did recognise you,' I said under my breath. 'What was the trial?'

Her expression hardened. 'He was convicted of the sexual assault of a fifteen-year-old girl when he worked as a teaching assistant at a school in Buckley. And of making and distributing pornographic images of young girls. It's all coming back to me now. The school had failed to carry out a full DBS check, and he had prior convictions for this type of offence.'

'Jesus,' I groaned angrily. It was a mistake exactly like that which could lead to another disaster like the one in Soham, Suffolk, in 2002 when Ian Huntley had managed to evade various checks, secured employment as a school caretaker, and then murdered two ten-year-old girls, Holly Wells and Jessica Chapman.

'I sentenced Tinsdale to nine years. He's now permanently on the sex offenders' register. He left prison on licence in 2011. No further offences recorded.'

'No wonder he was rattled when he realised where he knew you from,' I said.

We came over the brow of a hill, and the rugged landscape of Eryri stretched out. There were tiny dots where sheep were doing their best to find grass through the snow. A road sign read *Harlech 10 miles*.

'Doesn't help us get access to that video though, does it?' she pointed out.

But I'd already had a thought.

'It might do, actually.'

'Really? His licence has expired and he hasn't committed any crimes as far as we know.'

'He works for a plumbing company,' I pointed out, 'and technically plumbers have to have a basic DBS check. There's no guarantee that a small plumbing company in North Wales would have carried that out.'

Annie narrowed her eyes and looked over at me with an amused expression. 'I hope you're not suggesting that we use the threat of going to his employers with his past convictions to get us leverage and access to that video?'

I gave her a wink. 'That's exactly what I'm suggesting we do.'

Chapter 27

'And this is me and Marcus out in the Gulf,' Ollie Cannon said as he pointed to a large framed photo that hung on the wall in the hallway of his neat and tidy home.

Annie and I had arrived there about ten minutes ago and, unlike Robert Tinsdale, he was more than happy to talk to us about Marcus. In fact, he was friendly and welcoming.

I peered at the photo of the platoon who were standing in their desert camouflage with tents and sand dunes behind them. It was dated *28th August 1990*.

'We were still bloody teenagers,' Ollie said, shaking his head. He looked upset and wiped his eyes. 'Sorry. It's just that Marcus' death has been such a shock.'

'No need to apologise,' Annie reassured him with a sympathetic look.

'My wife and kids ... well, I say kids, they're both in their late 20s now. They're out shopping. Sales. Can't think of anything worse.' He said this with a smile, but the weight of Marcus' death was still on him.

'No,' I agreed. 'Torture.'

He gestured to a door in the hallway. 'Why don't you come and sit in here? Sorry, where are my manners? Would you like a coffee or tea?'

I shook my head. 'Thanks, but we're fine.'

Annie and I went into a tastefully decorated living room. The walls had been painted a subtle green, thick carpets, big sofa, and lots of cushions and rugs.

We sat down on the sofa and nearly disappeared into it.

Ollie frowned as he sat down in an armchair. 'You said you were looking into Marcus' death? I don't really understand.'

I started to explain. 'Richard Daniels is a very old friend of mine …'

Ollie nodded and chipped in. 'He's a top bloke. I can't imagine what he's going through. I know he's not been well recently.'

'That's right,' I replied. 'I happened to be riding past Marcus' home on New Year's Day when Sian found him. I'm an ex-detective with the North Wales Police. I wasn't convinced by what I saw and found that Marcus hadn't actually taken his own life.'

'What?' Ollie squinted in confusion. 'Sorry, but I still don't understand.'

'We think someone else might be involved,' Annie said.

'Oh God.' He looked horrified. 'You think someone did that to him?'

'Possibly.'

He shook his head in disbelief. 'Jesus Christ. You mean someone might have killed him?'

I nodded.

'Why?' Ollie asked with a deep frown.

Annie leaned forward. 'You were with Marcus on New Year's Eve morning and afternoon. Is that right?'

'Yeah. I'd taken the dogs over there. We walked up to

those ruins, then we had a spot of lunch and I headed back here late afternoon.'

I rubbed my chin. 'How did he seem?'

'Fine,' he replied without hesitation. 'He was on bloody good form actually.'

'He had been suspended from school, hadn't he?'

'Yeah, but he didn't seem that bothered about it to be honest. Said it was all gonna blow over. Said that everyone knew the girl was a liar and had a screw loose.' Then his face dropped. 'Christ, you don't think what happened with that girl had anything to do with it, do you? Marcus mentioned the girl's dad had a pop at him in the school car park a few weeks ago, but he could still handle himself and he wasn't scared of anyone.'

'We're not sure,' Annie replied, 'but we don't think so.'

'But we are looking for anything or anyone that might have put Marcus in danger,' I stated. 'Can you think of anything?'

He thought for a few seconds and then shook his head. 'No, nothing. You see we were both getting geared up to launch another appeal over our Gulf War Syndrome compensation claim.'

'I was part of the legal team that looked at the original compensation case against the MOD in 2005,' Annie told him.

'Were you? Sorry, I'm terrible with faces.'

'Don't worry,' she said with a half smile. 'It was nearly twenty years ago.'

Something about what Ollie had said sparked my interest. 'How far had you and Marcus got with this?'

'Quite a long way actually.' He stood up and went over to some shelves. 'We'd found legal representation. Patrick Adams QC?'

Annie nodded. 'I know Patrick. He's very good but he's very expensive.'

Ollie took a folder from the shelves. 'Patrick was willing to do it pro bono. I know that's very unusual for someone like him, but his brother fought in Afghanistan and his son is a lawyer in the army.' He sat back down and put the folder on the coffee table. 'It's all in that folder. I can make you copies if you want?'

'Yes, that would be useful,' Annie said.

'We had a lot more medical data about Gulf War Syndrome,' Ollie explained. 'More ex-soldiers who had symptoms. More medical experts who said that these symptoms were a result of Iranian nerve gas. Patrick thought we had a really good chance of getting compensation this time. And of course there's over three thousand of us, so the MOD's compensation bill would run into tens of millions.'

I gave Annie a meaningful look. Was there something in this that linked to Marcus being murdered?

'Had you contacted the MOD?' I asked.

'Oh yes. Patrick had made an initial contact and said that they were definitely rattled. The bastards had thought we'd gone away.'

'Was there a hearing date?' Annie asked.

'Next month. That's what Marcus and I were talking about when we took the dogs for a walk. He was so fired up about it. That's why it didn't make any sense to me when Sian called to say that he'd taken his life that night.'

'Yes. That seems to be the general opinion.'

Ollie's face then dropped. 'Hold on. You don't think that our case against the MOD has anything to do with what happened to him do you?'

'It wasn't even on our radar until ten minutes ago, to be honest,' I remarked.

Annie was deep in thought. 'If the MOD thought that they were going to be paying out tens of millions, who knows what lengths they might go to to stop that happening?'

I looked at her. It sounded a little far-fetched but it was something that needed to be investigated.

Chapter 28

Annie and I had been driving for half an hour, both deep in thought about what Ollie had told us. My first task was to go back and 'gently persuade' Tinsdale to let us in and give us the video his doorbell had recorded on New Year's Eve. I had no idea if his reluctance to let us in was connected to him resuming his previous criminal behaviour, or just a wariness of letting any strangers into his house. I presumed that if you were a convicted paedophile and distributor of illegal pornography, you would by nature be cautious and secretive.

Annie had been talking on the phone. She had been trying to contact Patrick Adams QC, the legal counsel who Marcus and Ollie had engaged for their compensation claim.

She ended the call and turned to me. 'I finally managed to track him down. I guess everyone is still on holiday at the moment.'

'Will he meet us?' I asked hopefully.

'He's in the middle of playing golf at Llangollen Golf Club. To be fair, he was pretty gracious about the fact that

I'd interrupted him. He said if we can get to the bar in about two hours' time, he's more than happy to run through stuff with us.'

'Great,' I said with a nod.

'Is this really a line we're pursuing?' she asked, sounding sceptical.

'I know it all sounds a bit like some terrible Hollywood film,' I admitted.

'Yes it does, which is why I feel it's very far-fetched,' she said sternly.

'I'm just going on trace, interview, and eliminate,' I said with a shrug. 'It could still have been O'Dowd and Morris. We don't know it's not either of them for sure.'

'But it seems highly unlikely.'

'But not impossible,' I added, 'and we have Glynis who has more than enough motive and anger to have wanted to harm her brother. But it would have required someone to help her. We've no idea if her husband, David, is the sort of man who would help to kill his own brother-in-law.'

'Not forgetting Marcus' wife, Sian,' Annie pointed out. 'We do have the strange fact that her brother Owen might have been at the cottage when you arrived on New Year's Day morning but made no appearance.'

'Does Sian have motive to kill Marcus?' I asked, acting as devil's advocate.

'He's been suspended from school for alleged inappropriate behaviour towards a seventeen-year-old girl. Hardly makes him husband of the year, does it?'

'Except I get the distinct feeling that those allegations are going to be found to be bogus. Of course, I don't know that for certain. More importantly, if Sian thought there was any credence in it, she might have lost her temper. And maybe her brother helped her?'

'It wasn't a crime of passion or loss of control though,

was it? It was a cold, calculated killing that required careful planning,' Annie pointed out.

'Yes, that's true.'

As I looked up, I saw Tinsdale's cottage looming into view. The sun glinted off the snowy fields and I had to squint as I slowed down to park outside. His plumber's van was still outside so he hadn't decided to vanish after our visit, which was a relief.

We strolled along the road and then up the path through the garden. As we got to the front door, it struck me that there was a possibility that he would use his video doorbell, see that it was me and Annie, and then refuse to answer the door.

I pressed the doorbell, took a step back, and waited.

Nothing.

Annie gave me a withering look.

I stepped forward and gave the door a loud bang. I wasn't prepared to leave until we'd spoken to Tinsdale and got that video.

'I was afraid this was going to happen,' Annie muttered under her breath as she moved across to the downstairs window, cupped her hands, and peered inside. Then she rapped her ring loudly against the glass. 'Mr Tinsdale, we know you're in there. You need to open the door,' she shouted.

I gave the door several more loud bangs but I knew that we were going to have to do something more drastic.

'Right, fuck this,' I growled angrily as I marched down the path. 'I'll be back in a second.'

I walked to my truck, reached under the tarpaulin, rummaged through some tools and then grabbed a heavy iron crowbar.

I marched back towards Tinsdale's cottage.

Annie's eyes widened. 'You're not going to break in

while he's in there? I'm not sure how we'd explain that if he calls the police.'

'He won't call the police,' I snorted, 'but that's not what I'm doing.'

I moved over to the plumber's van which had white and blue writing on the side.

'Oi, Bob!' I yelled at the top of my voice. 'Bob? I'm going to need you to come out here right now.'

I scanned the windows to see if he was looking out. He must have been there somewhere but I couldn't see him.

Taking the crowbar, I swung it back and smashed it into the wing mirror with a satisfying CRASH. Glass dropped onto the snow by my feet.

'Bob? I'm going to keep doing this until your van is a write-off and needs to be scrapped,' I thundered angrily.

Nothing. Annie gave me one of her looks.

'No?' I shouted. 'Okay.'

I swung the crowbar back and hit the driver's window with everything I had. The glass smashed, most of it falling into the van.

Glancing up, I saw Tinsdale looking out of a ground floor window from behind a curtain.

I then tapped the windscreen with the crowbar. 'Right, Bob, windscreen is next. Or you can just let us in and give us that video. You choose.'

As I swung the crowbar back, the front door opened and Tinsdale came scuttling out. 'All right, all right! You win, you bastard!' he shouted.

'Oh, I'm glad you see it like that,' I said with a smirk. He was a sex offender and I had no sympathy. Fuck him. He's lucky I didn't go and hit him with the crowbar for wasting our bloody time.

'Here,' he snapped as he held out a small black computer memory stick.

Annie snatched it from his hand and smiled. 'Thank you very much.'

I wandered over. 'Just so we're clear, Bob. If I find that the video footage from New Year's Eve night and the early hours of New Year's Day is not on that, I'll be ringing your employer and giving him a full and detailed CV about your time at Her Majesty's pleasure.'

Tinsdale sneered at me. 'Yeah, it's all on there. Don't worry.' He shuffled back into his cottage and slammed the door behind him.

Chapter 29

I took a tray of drinks from the bar in Llangollen Golf Club to the corner table where Annie and Patrick Adams were sitting.

Patrick was in his late 60s, handsome, clean-shaven, silver hair, and very well groomed.

'Here you go,' I said as I put the tray down on the table and handed out the drinks.

The bar was about half full. Mainly middle-aged to elderly men sitting and chatting.

'Cheers,' Patrick said as he clinked glasses with us. 'It's nice to see you, Annie. Been too long. I'm sorry that it's not in better circumstances.'

I assumed that while I'd waited at the bar, Annie had filled Patrick in with the details of Marcus' death, our suspicions, and the conversation we'd had with Ollie Cannon.

'Could you briefly fill Frank in with what you've told me?' Annie asked.

'Of course,' Patrick said. 'As I explained to Annie, Marcus and Ollie had first contacted me about two years ago. It was just a preliminary chat about the legal compensation case from back in 2004 and 2005.'

'But you weren't involved with that original case?' I asked.

'No, but I'd kept my eye on it. I come from an army family - father, brother, son - and I'd heard all the stories about Gulf War Syndrome.' He gestured to Annie. 'To be honest, I thought that the MOD would have to pay out but, as Annie said, it was a whitewash.'

'What do you guys mean when you say whitewash?' I asked, wanting to get a clearer picture.

Annie moved closer to the table and put her glass down. 'Medical experts who appeared from nowhere that we hadn't been told about. Professors who suddenly came out of the woodwork to give their views on nerve gases and symptoms.'

Patrick sat forward and lowered his voice. 'Then there was the whole thing about the group claim losing their right to legal aid,' he reminded Annie.

'Yes. Once they'd lost their right to legal aid, they were effectively on a sinking ship,' she explained. 'I suspected there were some very underhand dealings going on in Whitehall to make sure that they lost legal aid.'

'Of course,' Patrick agreed, raising his eyebrow knowingly. 'The compensation would have run to millions. And it would have been a PR disaster for the MOD, the British Army and the government.'

Annie moved closer to us and lowered her voice to a whisper. 'Then we had reports that a few ex-servicemen not only withdrew their compensation claim, but also went on record to admit that they had exaggerated their symptoms. Rumour had it that they had been leaned on or paid off.'

I sighed. 'Jesus.' I hadn't known the extent to which the

MOD had gone to avoid the compensation claim. 'All very clandestine stuff.'

'The MOD have got form for this kind of thing,' Patrick said wearily. 'They went to the High Court in 2009 to try to reduce compensation because so many soldiers were being sent back home from Afghanistan. It was disgusting.'

Annie looked over at me. 'A couple of years ago, the MOD brought out a new policy, *Better Combat Compensation*. They used the smokescreen of army pensions to hide the fact that they were doing everything in their power to stop claims of negligence coming to court.'

'It was a bloody farce,' Patrick said with anger. 'It effectively stopped the MOD and the British Government being liable for any injuries on a battlefield, even if there had been negligence. Complete joke.'

Realising that we were getting a little sidetracked into a discussion of the MOD's questionable legal policies, I said, 'Have you filled Patrick in about our suspicions regarding Marcus' death?'

Annie nodded. 'Briefly.'

'What do you think, Patrick?'

'Marcus was about to open up a whole new can of worms with this compensation case. It was my feeling that we would win if we went to court with it.' Then he leaned across the table. 'Listen, I've been around long enough to see the MOD resort to some very ruthless and immoral tactics to get what they perceive to be the right outcome. You only have to look at what happened in Ireland. They sanctioned torture and murder over there. And you've seen what the SAS were allowed to do in Afghanistan. In my opinion, the MOD are capable of doing anything to get what they want. And if that means faking someone's suicide to stop a seventy-five million pound compensation claim, then I couldn't rule that out.'

I exchanged a dark look with Annie. Had we suddenly opened up some kind of state-sponsored murder by looking into Marcus' death?

Chapter 30

Annie and I were in my office at the farmhouse. I pulled over a chair for her to sit on and grabbed my laptop.

'Here you go,' she said, as she handed me the memory stick from Tinsdale.

Our conversation with Patrick at the golf club had certainly given us food for thought, but it had also taken our investigation into a whole new arena. If Annie and I started to dig around in some kind of covert MOD operation, it would put us in great danger.

I pushed the memory stick into a slot on my laptop.

I looked over at Annie. She'd been through enough in the past three months, and it didn't seem fair to drag her into something this dangerous.

'Maybe we should back off on this?' I suggested.

She met my gaze. 'Back off?' she said dismissively. 'I've never seen you want to 'back off' from anything in your life, Frank.'

'I'm worried that I'm getting you into something far riskier and more dangerous than we first thought it might be.'

'No. We can't stop now,' she said resolutely. 'In fact, the stuff that Patrick told us makes me more determined to find out what happened to Marcus. And if there is some kind of MOD involvement, we need to expose it.'

I pulled a face. 'That's easier said than done ... and neither of us are spring chickens.'

'Speak for yourself, mate,' she laughed.

I held up my hands in defeat. 'Okay, okay. I just want us to go into this with our eyes wide open.'

She pointed at my laptop. 'Stop fussing and let's see what's on that video.'

I gave her a wry smile. 'You're definitely getting bossier the older you get.'

She gave me the finger. 'Yes, well as you pointed out, I don't have the time to faff about as I'm so bloody old.'

'Okay, point taken,' I conceded with a grin as I went onto my laptop. I clicked on a few files and then tried to find where the memory stick was located. 'Hmm, I'm getting a bit stuck trying to find this thing.'

She moved her chair nearer, put on her reading glasses, and peered at the screen. 'Mind if I ...' she asked, as she leaned closer.

'I think it's on this drive here,' she said as she moved the attached mouse around. 'Oh dear.'

I chuckled. 'Oh god, it's the blind leading the blind here, isn't it?'

'Here we go, you miserable bugger,' she said triumphantly.

'Great,' I said. 'Now let's see what's on there.'

I clicked on the video file that was marked *31.12.22. // 01.01.23.*

The screen filled with the image from Tinsdale's doorbell camera; his garden path, front garden, and the road beyond that.

The timecode read *00.13am*.

'Right, well we need to be right at the end of this, don't we?' I said under my breath as I started to move the cursor along the timeline at the bottom of the screen.

As the timecode got to *23.00* I stopped, and started to play the video forward at X2 speed.

'I don't think we need to go any earlier than this, do we?' I asked Annie.

'No,' she agreed, as we both peered intently at the screen.

Then her phone rang and she glanced down at it.

'Ooh, I'd better take this,' she said knowingly. 'I've pulled a few strings to get this phone call ... Hello?'

She wandered out of my office into the hallway, and I continued to watch the video as it played forward. It had now reached *23.55pm*, but apart from a few passing cars there had been nothing of interest.

The timecode passed midnight, but I remembered from what Sian had told me, Marcus had gone outside for a smoke at about 12.30am.

As the timecode reached *00.38am*, a car came into view and then stopped in the middle of the road.

It was a black Range Rover Sport.

I paused the image. *That's weird.*

Pressing play again, I watched as the car stayed motionless on the road for about ten seconds. Then it pulled forward very slowly before jerking away at high speed.

It looked very suspicious to me but, because of the angle of the doorbell and only the driver's side being in full view, it was hard to see from the footage if the car had dropped someone off from the passenger side.

Whatever was going on, it was incredibly suspicious

given that it tied in very closely to the time we believed that Marcus had been killed.

Playing the footage back, I got to where the car first entered the frame and paused it.

I grabbed a pen and a post-it note, and jotted down the registration number – *TD21 BNB*. I'd contact Kelly and see if she could run the plate for us.

'What have we got?' Annie asked as she came back into the office.

I played the footage back and showed her.

'Definitely suspicious. We need to run the plate.' Then she frowned, leaned nearer to the screen, and pointed. 'What's that?'

I moved closer and saw what she was pointing to. The headlights of another car which seemed to be parked across the driveway of the Daniels' house.

'Who's that?' she asked.

'I can't read the plate from here, or even see what type of car it is,' I said in frustration, 'but it looks like someone is waiting there.'

'Could it be Sian's brother's car?' she suggested.

'He's got an old-fashioned Land Rover Defender, but I can't make it out from this. We need to find someone who can clean up the image.'

She shot me a look. 'Ethan?'

I nodded and then indicated her phone. 'You been pulling strings again?'

'We've got a meeting with the MOD's legal counsel. Barracks are in Wrexham.'

Chapter 31

As I sped up the A483 bypass towards Wrexham, I noticed that there was a car behind us. It had been there since we'd come through Corwen and then Llangollen.

A black Range Rover Sport.

Reaching up, I adjusted my rear-view mirror to keep the car in view.

'Everything all right?' Annie asked, noticing my distraction.

'I'm not sure yet.'

With a burst of speed, I pulled out into the outer lane and sped up to 80mph. I overtook about half a dozen cars before pulling back into the inside lane.

With my eyes fixed on the Range Rover, I saw it manoeuvre out, speed up past the same cars and then pull in, leaving one car between us. Whoever it was, they weren't stupid enough to sit directly behind me.

'Don't look round, but I've got a feeling that we're being followed,' I said calmly as I checked the Range Rover's position in my rear-view mirror again.

'Really?' Annie moved in her seat so she could see behind us using the wing mirror on her side.

I gave her a meaningful look. 'Black Range Rover Sport.'

She nodded. 'Yes, I see it. I can't see the licence plate though.'

'No,' I said.

Looking ahead, I saw that the turning to Rhosllanerchrugog – or Rhos as it was commonly known – was coming up.

I pulled out into the outer lane without indicating and slammed down on the accelerator.

Annie and I were jolted back in our seats as the truck's powerful engine roared and we sped up to 80mph and then 90mph.

We overtook two lorries.

I had my eyes locked onto the turning from the A483 to Rhos which was fast approaching.

Flicking my eyes to the rear-view mirror, I spotted that the Range Rover had pulled out again. It was about 40 to 50 yards behind us.

'Ready to hold on tight?' I asked Annie.

'Erm, do I have a choice?' she asked anxiously.

'No.'

I slammed the brakes on.

Then I swerved the truck into the small space between the two lorries.

We'd slowed to only 40mph in a matter of seconds.

Then with a quick turn of the steering wheel, I pulled the truck left onto the exit for Rhos which led down to a roundabout.

I glanced in the mirror again and saw that the Range Rover had tried to do the same.

After a couple of seconds, it appeared on the road behind us.

'Yeah, we're definitely being followed,' I said to Annie.

Coming to a stop at the roundabout, I waited for the Range Rover to come up behind us. They had no choice now.

'Okay, here we go,' I said under my breath as it slowed down.

I got a clear view of the licence plate – *TD21 BNB*.

As I pulled out onto the roundabout, I glanced across at Annie. 'It's the same car that we saw pull up outside Tinsdale and Daniels' cottages on New Year's Eve. The one on the video. Same plate.'

Annie looked concerned.

As we headed into Wrexham, I grabbed my phone and tapped in the number for DS Kelly Thomas.

The phone rang through Bluetooth.

'Hello, DS Thomas?' said a voice.

'Kelly? It's Frank Marshal. Sorry, I know you'd prefer me not to call you at work but we've got a bit of a situation here.'

'What kind of situation?' she asked cautiously.

'We're being followed by a black Range Rover Sport,' I explained. 'We're in Wrexham and it's followed us all the way from Snowdonia. It's the same car we saw on Tinsdale's doorbell video. It stopped outside the Daniels' cottage at 12.38am on New Year's Day morning.'

'How do you know it's the same car, Frank?' she asked.

'Same plate. We got it from the video. It's the same car that's now sitting behind us.'

'Can you give me the number so I can run it through the PNC?'

'Of course. It's Tango, Delta, Two, One, Bravo, November, Bravo.'

'Okay, Frank, leave it with me. I'll get back to you. Why are you in Wrexham, by the way?'

'We're meeting an army legal counsel,' I said. 'Probably better that I explain it to you face to face.'

'Probably. I'll get back to you about that car. If you think you're in danger, call me and I can get local units to help out.'

'Thanks, Kelly,' I said as I ended the call.

'We're here,' Annie said, pointing to the entrance of the MOD Army Barracks in Hightown, Wrexham.

There was a large red dragon emblem on the wall with a sign *The Royal Welsh*. On the other side of the gates was a black banner – *101 Force Support Battalion – RECRUITING NOW!*

I glanced in the rear-view mirror again. The Range Rover had vanished.

We got to the barrier and a young soldier came to our window.

Annie told him who we were meeting, the barrier lifted, and we drove in.

Chapter 32

Having parked, signed in at reception and then been given security passes, we were escorted by a young female soldier to Andrew Peterman, a top MOD lawyer. Annie had pulled strings and used her reputation in the legal world to get a meeting. I was astounded that Peterman, who was a QC, had agreed to meet us.

We walked briskly along the long dark corridor that had various photos of platoons and regiments on the wall, along with a series of photos of soldiers who had been lost in combat.

We arrived at a large oak door and the female soldier knocked loudly.

'Come in,' boomed a voice from the office.

The soldier opened the door, gestured for us to go in, and then closed the door behind us.

The room was musty and smelled like an old library. The walls were covered floor to ceiling with book shelves full of hard-backed books, folders, and files. To our right was a large picture of King Charles III on the wall. It had only been four months since the death of Elizabeth II.

Over to our left, a regimental badge and Latin motto were attached to the wall.

Peterman, 40s, slim, straw-blond hair, blue eyes, got up immediately and came over to shake our hands.

'Justice Taylor,' he said. 'It's good to finally meet you.'

'I've retired I'm afraid,' Annie said as she and I settled into two leather armchairs in front of Peterman's enormous oak desk. 'It's just Annie now.'

Peterman settled in the seat behind his desk. 'Well, your reputation precedes you.' I wondered how long he was going to continue to be this obsequious once he knew why we were there.

'You're probably wondering why we're here?' Annie said, and then gestured to me. 'This is a good friend of mine, Frank Marshall.'

Peterman nodded a hello to me. Then he shrugged. 'I assumed that it's something to do with the Gulf War Syndrome compensation case. I've just been put in charge of the MOD's defence counsel. I know you were on the original legal team that presented the claim back in 2004. I just assumed that you were here because of that, although I wasn't quite sure why.'

'It is connected to that,' Annie confirmed. 'I wonder if you're familiar with the names Marcus Daniels or Ollie Cannon?'

Peterman paused for a second and searched his memory. 'Yes. I believe that Marcus Daniels is the ex-serviceman who has launched this new compensation claim?'

I nodded and looked over at him. 'Yes, that's right. He was.' I'd been watching Peterman ever since we'd walked in, and there was nothing that endeared me to him. He seemed like an archetypal, entitled English public school wanker.

He looked confused. 'Was? Has he dropped out of the case or …'

'No. I'm afraid he's dead,' Annie said sharply.

'Dead? Gosh, erm, I had no idea,' he bumbled. 'How dreadful.'

'Someone made it look as if he took his own life,' I said sternly, 'but he didn't. He was murdered.'

'Surely the police are looking into this?' he asked.

I sighed. 'You would think they would be, wouldn't you?'

He sat forward at his desk and looked at Annie. 'Well, I'm terribly sorry to hear about Mr Daniels and …'

Annie interrupted him. 'You see, Marcus Daniels was the driving force behind the new compensation claim. Just as he was back in 2004. Except someone has killed him. And it's a serious setback to the compensation claim as a whole.'

Peterman furrowed his brow. 'I'm sorry, but you can't seriously be suggesting that Mr Daniels' alleged murder and this new compensation claim are in any way linked?'

I fixed the pompous dickhead with a stare. 'Are they?' I asked.

'Come on,' he laughed.

'Please don't laugh Andrew. This isn't remotely funny,' Annie snapped.

'No, not funny. But absurd,' he said defensively.

'The MOD stands to lose up to seventy-five million pounds if this claim is successful,' I said accusingly. 'It seems to be a huge coincidence that a few weeks after that claim is lodged with the MOD, the principal driving force behind it is killed in very suspicious circumstances.'

Peterman shook his head. 'I think you both need to be very careful bandying around crackpot theories like that.'

'Is that a threat?' I asked indignantly.

His whole demeanour had changed in the past few minutes. 'No, not a threat. But I'm sure neither of you are naïve enough to think that you can take on the MOD in something like this.'

'Why? Are we in danger if we do, Andrew?' Annie asked coldly.

For a few seconds, he didn't answer. Then he laughed. 'Of course not. I meant legally, Annie.'

'Have you got a car following us?' I asked, looking for his reaction.

'A car?' he mumbled as he got up from his chair. 'Not that I'm aware of.'

'That's not a definitive 'no' though is it?' Annie said.

Peterman came out from behind his desk. 'I think that our meeting is concluded.' He opened the door and signalled to the female soldier who was waiting in the corridor. 'Private Callaghan will show you out.'

Chapter 33

Annie and I used our gloved hands to sweep the remnants of the snow from the picnic bench near the car park at Coed y Brenin Forest Park. In Welsh it meant *King's Forest*.

I took a moment to look down at my phone and check the GPS tracker that I had attached to TJ's car. It was still parked on his drive which was a relief.

Then I watched a family arrive and park their 4x4. They had their mountain bikes attached to racks on the rear of the car. The man I assumed to be the father got out of the driver's side, went round to the back, and started to unclip the bikes.

'I used to bring James here with his bike,' I said quietly, realising that I hadn't thought of that for many years.

Annie looked at me. 'You must miss him so much. Even now.'

'Yeah.' I nodded. 'You know what sometimes scares me the most?'

She shook her head.

'That James will be forgotten. That people will just forget all about him once Rachel and I are gone.' I tried to still the emotion in my voice. 'I can't bear to think about that. Rachel and I have Caitlin and Sam. We've made some kind of mark on the world. But James never did. He didn't have time to. Does that make sense?'

'That makes perfect sense,' Annie said gently.

'I guess that's why when someone dies young there are competitions, cups, or trophies named after them so that they aren't forgotten,' I said, thinking out loud. 'But James won't have that. I don't know what the answer is.' I gestured to the 4x4. 'Seeing that guy there unclipping the mountain bikes just reminded me.'

There was a poignant silence for a few seconds and then I saw Kelly approaching. She'd called me half an hour ago asking to meet face to face as it was urgent.

'She's here,' I said.

Kelly shivered as she approached. 'Hi there.'

'Maybe we should meet somewhere indoors next time,' I joked, but I could see from Kelly's expression that she wasn't really in a jovial mood.

I reached over and swept the rest of the snow from the picnic bench so that she could sit down.

'Anything on TJ?' I asked, even though I knew she was meeting us to talk about Marcus' murder.

'CID at Dolgellau have set up surveillance on his cottage. We've got a meeting with the NCA as they've got a firearms operation somewhere in North Wales and don't know if it's linked.'

The National Crime Agency (NCA) was a national division of the UK police force. It dealt specifically with organised crime gangs (OCGs) and investigated drug, weapon, and human trafficking.

'Okay,' I said gratefully. 'Thanks for letting me know.'

'That's fine,' Kelly said, 'but obviously that's not why I wanted to meet you here.'

Annie turned towards her. 'I take it this is not good news?'

She shook her head 'No.'

Then she looked at me. 'I ran that plate you gave me.'

'And?' I asked.

'For starters, it's got a very restricted access on it.'

Annie frowned. 'Why?'

Kelly gave us both a dark look. 'It's an MOD car, although it's actually owned by a private security firm, Valley Security.'

My stomach tensed as I took a breath. 'Who the hell are Valley Security?'

Kelly took out her phone and showed us a photo of a very tough-looking man with dark cropped hair and a moustache. 'They're owned by this man. Terry Palmer. Ex-SAS, Special Forces. Served in Afghanistan. Now he's a private contractor.' She flicked to another photo of a bully of a man with a shaved head. 'This is his main sidekick, Ashley Harris. Basically Palmer, and everyone who works for him, are mercenaries for hire. Protection for ships in Somalia. Diplomatic protection service in the Middle East and South America.'

'Jesus,' I said, shaking my head. 'You've seen the video of the car I sent over?'

'Yes,' she replied. 'I'm sorry, Frank, but this is way above my pay scale. I think that if you and Annie continue to dig around into Marcus' death, you're in grave danger.'

Annie was angry. 'What are we supposed to do? Just ignore what we've found out?'

Kelly seemed a little lost. 'Honestly I just don't know, but I'm going to have to take this to my superiors. I'd lose my job if I didn't.'

I nodded. 'Of course. I understand that, but I'm scared that once it's passed up, everyone is going to close ranks and Marcus' death is going to get swept under the carpet.'

'There's just no evidence though, Frank,' Kelly pointed out. 'It's highly suspicious that this car stopped outside and then drove off, but I didn't see anyone get out of it. And we only have your word that the stepladder was in the wrong place and had mud on the top steps. Even the Chief Pathologist can't confirm that Marcus was injected with anything untoward. There's nothing to go on apart from your and Annie's instinct that something is wrong.'

'What do you think, Kelly?' Annie asked in a measured tone. 'Do you think that Marcus took his own life?'

'I don't know what to think. I just know I'm way out of my depth with this.'

I let out an audible sigh. What Kelly had said was right. There was nothing concrete to go on.

Annie raised an eyebrow. 'What about involving an investigative journalist? I've got a few contacts.'

Kelly shrugged as she got up from the bench. 'If you two want to go down that route I can't stop you. But please be careful. Terry Palmer is a very dangerous man. And so is everyone who works for him, especially Harris.'

Chapter 34

Driving slowly out of Coed y Brenin Forest Park, I looked out at the dense trees that still had a dusting of snow on them. The sun glistened off their branches. But it was hard to concentrate on anything after our conversation with Kelly.

'You were a police officer for a very long time, Frank,' Annie said after a while. 'Have you ever heard of anything like this before?'

I thought for a few seconds. 'Actually, we did have something back in the mid-80s. There was a Labour MP, Selwyn Williams, based in North Wales. There were a lot of rumours that he was part of Militant Tendency.'

Militant Tendency was a Trotskyist group who infiltrated the Labour Party in the 1970s and 1980s. Some believed that MT posed the biggest threat of subversion in the UK since the Communist Party of Great Britain.

'I remember a lot of people getting their knickers in a twist over Militant Tendency back then,' Annie said.

'Selwyn Williams came to us claiming that he was being followed. He told us that it was MI5,' I continued, 'then his flat up in Colwyn was burgled. When CID went to have a look, nothing of value had been taken. But some of his Labour Party documents and folders had been stolen.'

Annie frowned. 'Which is very suspicious.'

'The more CID looked into it, the more we got the feeling that MI5 were involved. Then our superintendent had a quiet, off the record, word to say that Whitehall had been in touch and that we weren't to investigate anything that Williams reported to us.'

'Jesus,' Annie sighed. 'Unfortunately, that doesn't surprise me. Back in the 90s, I had a pre-trial hearing in which a very prominent Peer of the Realm was accused of historic sexual abuse against underage boys. A trial date was set with the CPS, but within weeks the case was dropped. Several witnesses had withdrawn their evidence, and a CPS lawyer told me they had been pressured by Whitehall to make it go away.'

Although I was listening to Annie's story, I was preoccupied by a vehicle coming up behind me at speed.

Daylight was fading and the roads through Eryri National Park were thick with fog.

'Everything okay?' Annie asked, noticing that I was distracted.

My eyes were focused on the rear-view mirror. 'I'm not sure yet.'

Then I saw blazing headlights.

For a moment, I was dazzled.

'Shit,' I hissed.

It was the same black Range Rover Sport.

I took a long breath in. 'As they say in all good westerns, we've got company.'

Annie turned around to look. 'Frankly I don't care if

they see me turn around. We know they're following us and we know who they are.'

The Range Rover sped up so that it was very close behind me.

My pulse started to quicken. *What the hell are they doing that for?*

Looking forward, the visibility on the winding country road was down to twenty yards due to the fog. I couldn't go any faster or we'd be in danger of coming off the road or colliding with traffic coming the other way.

The Range Rover was so close that I could see its number plate.

Suddenly, there was a BANG.

Annie and I were jolted forward.

The car had rammed into the back of us.

What the hell?

'Oh my God!' Annie yelled, clutching the back of her neck.

'You okay?' I asked, now filled with a mixture of fear and rage.

'What the hell are they doing?'

I stamped down on the accelerator.

My eyes were now flicking between the foggy road ahead and the Range Rover behind.

We came hammering around a bend too fast and I had to grip the steering wheel. I felt the back tyres slip a little.

'We're in the middle of nowhere,' Annie pointed out.

I heard the Range Rover engine revving as it came speeding up behind us again.

BANG!

This time the force of the jolt meant I lost control of the truck momentarily.

'Jesus!' I snarled. 'Bastards.'

Annie looked terrified. 'What do we do?' she asked anxiously.

'I'm not sure,' I admitted as we went over the top of the hill and down the other side. 'My shotgun's at home, and I suspect that they're armed.'

'What are they going to do? Kidnap us?'

I handed Annie my phone. 'Ring Kelly.'

She looked at the screen. 'No signal.'

'Bollocks.'

Glancing in my rear-view mirror, I saw that the Range Rover was now swerving behind us.

Looking ahead, I saw two sets of headlights coming the other way through the fog. Two cars were heading our way, but I didn't want to get anyone innocent involved or hurt.

Out of the corner of my eye, I saw the Range Rover was now out on the other side of the road. They were attempting to drive parallel to us.

I assumed they were going to ram us off the road from the side.

With a sudden roar, the Range Rover accelerated so that it was parallel.

'Frank!' Annie warned me.

'It's okay,' I tried to reassure her.

Glancing right, I saw a man sitting in the passenger seat.

30s, shaved head, squashed nose. I recognised him from the photo that Kelly had shown us. Ashley Harris.

He was smoking one of those cigarillos – short, thin cigars – as if he didn't have a care in the world.

What a wanker!

Our eyes met.

I gave him a wink. I wasn't going to let him know that I was actually scared.

'Hold on tight, Annie.'

'Why?' she asked.

'Annie! I said. 'Just do it!'

Then I stamped on the brake.

The tyres squealed and screamed under us as we skidded and the truck's wheels locked.

The Range Rover continued along the road for a few seconds.

It was exactly what I intended.

My knuckles were white as I gripped the steering wheel.

The Range Rover slammed its brakes on.

Its red brake lights glared in the fog.

Finally, the truck came to a stop.

The Range Rover skidded to a halt about fifty yards in front of us.

Looking ahead, I saw the two cars now approaching were slowing as their way was blocked.

The Range Rover turned across the road violently to get out of their way, and then sped away into the fog.

I tried to catch my breath for a few seconds.

Then I glanced at Annie who was shaking.

'It's okay,' I whispered. 'They've gone.'

She let out an exaggerated sigh. 'For now.'

Chapter 35

'Beer?' Annie asked me as I sat in her kitchen.

'Please,' I replied, 'unless you've got something stronger?'

'Scotch?'

'Perfect.'

She took a glass from the cupboard and held it up. 'I've only just stopped shaking.'

I stared at her for a long moment. 'I think this has to stop now, don't you?' I didn't want to stop our investigation into Marcus' death but the stakes were too high. And my concern was for Annie's safety.

'Sod that,' she snapped angrily. 'I'm not going to be bullied by some ex-army goons.'

I gave her an ironic smile. 'I admire your chutzpah, but aren't we being a bit foolhardy?'

'I'm pretty sure you can't actually be 'foolhardy' in your 70s.'

'Can't you?'

'No. It's a young person's thing. Like being reckless,'

she replied. 'When you get to our age, it's just getting on with life and making the most of the time we have left.'

'Yeah, well we might not have much time left at this rate,' I felt obliged to add.

'I'm surprised you'd allow yourself to be bullied by a bunch of English toffs, Frank.'

'Are you trying to provoke me into doing what you want me to do?' I asked with an amused expression.

She laughed. 'Obviously.'

'Well, can I remind you that these English toffs are trained by the SAS and are expert killers?'

'Pah.' She shrugged and then gave me a more serious look. 'I'm joking of course, but I'm not sure I can walk away from this without knowing what actually happened to Marcus. I think we owe it to him and his family.'

'I agree with you,' I conceded. 'I just don't want you to get hurt.'

'I can handle myself,' she pointed out. 'I saved your life three months ago, remember?'

I did remember. Her husband Stephen had been only seconds away from killing me when she stabbed him in the neck.

'I do remember,' I said, but before we could continue, my phone rang.

It was Ollie Cannon.

'Ollie?' I said with growing concern.

'Frank, sorry to call you …'

'Don't worry. What is it? I asked.

'I've been burgled.'

'When was this?'

'Just after lunch. We went out for a family walk with the dogs. By the time we got back, the place had been ransacked.'

'Annie and I will come over.'
'You don't need to do that,' he protested.
'We'll see you in about forty-five minutes.'

Chapter 36

'Jesus,' I said under my breath as Annie and I made our way into Ollie's home. It had been turned upside down.

'You called the police?' Annie asked.

'Of course,' Ollie replied. 'The wife and kids are so upset. They've gone to her mum's.'

'What did the police say?'

Ollie took a shaky breath. 'They didn't seem very fussed. Just a burglary.'

Annie raised an eyebrow. 'You don't look convinced?'

'It's just a bit strange,' he went on. 'TV is still here. Wife's laptop is on the kitchen table. They didn't even take her jewellery.'

I frowned and scratched at my chin. 'Did they take anything of value?'

'Not that I can see. The police said it was probably kids looking for cash.'

'Are they sending over anyone from CID?' I asked.

Ollie nodded. 'Probably not until tomorrow. And all they're going to do is dust for prints.'

'Probably,' I agreed.

Annie looked around. 'Any security cameras?'

'No.'

'Signs of a forced entry?' I asked, going over to the front door.

He thought for a few seconds then shook his head. 'Actually, no. The police officers didn't really pick up on it, but all the windows and doors are intact. I don't know how they got in.'

I gestured down the hallway to the kitchen. 'Mind if I have a look in there?'

'Of course not,' he said.

As I went into the kitchen, I could see that every drawer and cupboard had been opened and rummaged through.

Taking a step back, I saw the fading daylight coming through the window and hitting the tiled floor.

I crouched down, trying not to groan.

I squinted and could see a couple of faint footmarks on the tiled floor. Given their direction, they had come from the back door.

Standing up, I heard my knees crack – as they always did. I went over to the back door which led out to a patio and garden.

I leaned down and looked carefully at the door handle and lock.

'Where's the key to this door?' I asked.

Ollie pointed to a small wooden key rack over by the sink.

Twisting the handle, I opened the door and turned to Ollie who looked confused.

'You thought this was locked, didn't you?'

'It was locked. I definitely locked it before we all went

out, but I didn't even think to check it when we got back because it was closed.'

'I think that's what they were counting on.' I crouched down again and looked at the other side of the back door.

Where the handle and lock were located, there were the tell-tale metallic scratches on the surrounding area of the keyhole.

'Yeah, someone picked your lock from the outside,' I said, showing Ollie where the tools had scratched the metallic surround. 'You see these scratches here?'

'Picked the lock?' he said, a bewildered expression on his face.

'Not kids looking for cash then?' Annie said knowingly.

'Definitely not,' I said. 'They were professionals.'

Ollie gave me a dark look. 'You think this has something to do with this compensation claim, don't you?'

I gave a shrug. 'I'm not sure. Possibly.'

'Ollie, have you got any paperwork relevant to the new case that you and Marcus had lodged with Patrick Adams?' Annie asked.

'Yeah, in my study upstairs, but I didn't think to have a look for those.'

'Probably a good idea to go and check,' Annie suggested.

I pointed to the back garden. 'Have you got a back entrance to this place?'

'Yeah, over to the right. There's a tall gate that leads out to a little track where we leave our bins. Why?'

'I'm not sure yet,' I said, as Annie gave me a quizzical look.

Ollie marched out of the kitchen and down the hallway. 'I'll go and check for that stuff upstairs.'

'What are you thinking, Frank?' Annie asked.

I opened the back door wide and gestured for her to follow me out to the snow-covered garden.

Scanning the lawn, I could see that the snow was now getting a little patchy. At the far end of the garden was a small stone wall, and as I walked over to it I could see the edge of a footprint where there had been some attempt to cover it with snow.

'Someone has come over the back wall and walked across the lawn,' I said, thinking aloud. 'If it's those fuckers from the Range Rover, I assume they didn't want to park out the front and get spotted.'

There was also a newish-looking slatted wooden gate. The bolts at the top and bottom were both open.

I pointed to them. 'It's unlocked. If they'd come over the wall and left via this gate, there would be no way of locking the bolts on their exit.'

Opening the gate, I saw there was a single muddy, snowy track. Several houses seemed to back onto it and there were a couple of green wheely bins out.

Over to my right, there were deep tyre marks on the verge that had cut into the mud and snow.

'They look recent,' Annie remarked.

'They are,' I said, as my eyes scanned the ground. Then I saw something lying in the snow. Small and brown.

The butt from a cigarillo.

'Got you,' I said under my breath. I pointed to the cigarillo butt. 'The scumbag who was sat in the passenger seat of the Range Rover was smoking one of those cigarillos earlier.'

Annie glanced at me knowingly. 'Harris. So, it's definitely them?'

I nodded.

We went back through the gate, across the garden, and into the kitchen.

Ollie came jogging down the stairs, looking distraught.

'Every document related to the compensation claim has gone, and so has my laptop that I keep in a locked cabinet.'

Chapter 37

Taking a few heavy blocks of wood, I walked over to the roaring fire pit and chucked them in. The night sky above was inky black. I was deep in thought about the events of the day. So much had happened. I needed the evening just to process it all.

Sam was sitting to my left, huddled under a thick blanket.

'Warm enough, mate?' I asked as I went and sat beside him.

'Yes, Taid,' he said with a nod.

Jack sat at our feet, the flames reflecting in his dark brown eyes. I put my hand on his head and he looked up at me.

I took in a long deep breath of icy air and let it out with an audible sigh. 'Well, it's been a hell of a day, Sam. A hell of a day.'

He gave me a curious look. 'I thought you were retired. That's what Mum said.'

'So did I. So did I.' I gave a booming laugh and rubbed his head. 'Talking of which, where's your mother with those drinks?'

'Mum told me you shouldn't drink whiskey,' he said. He was referring to the fact that when Sam had requested a hot chocolate to drink by the fireside, I'd asked for any kind of whiskey.

I pointed at my chest. 'That I shouldn't drink whiskey?'

He thought for a second. 'No. She used to say that to my dad. She was always telling him that he drank too much whiskey and that it made him angry.'

'And did it?' I asked gently.

Sam didn't look at me but gave a little nod.

'Well, I'm sorry to hear that.' I put my hand on his shoulder. 'Do you miss your dad?'

'Sort of.' He shrugged and pulled a face. 'But he wasn't very nice to Mum.'

'Yeah, she told me.'

There was silence.

Caitlin came out with a tray. She was wearing a long puffa jacket, woolly hat, scarf and gloves.

'Jesus Dad, aren't you cold?' she said, shivering as she placed the tray down and then handed the drinks out.

'No,' I said, and then joked, 'You've gone soft since you moved north.'

'What does 'soft' mean?' Sam asked.

'I'm not sure. Weak?'

He looked confused. 'Can I toast some marshmallows on the fire, Mum?'

Caitlin nodded. 'If you can find some, you can.'

'Great.' He leapt to his feet with sudden energy and ran inside.

I laughed as I watched him.

For a few seconds, we sipped our drinks and looked at the dancing orange flames in the pit.

'Dad,' Caitlin said in a serious tone, 'there's something I need to talk to you about.'

'That sounds ominous,' I said with a wry smile.

'I don't think Sam and I should live here anymore. I think we should move somewhere else.'

'What?' I asked, shaking my head in bewilderment. I had no idea why she was saying this. 'Why?'

'This whole TJ thing,' she said softly. 'You've got Mum to look after. And even though it's horrible to say, she's going to get worse and need more support.'

'Caitlin, that's why I need you here. Your mum loves having you and Sam around. She's been a different person since you two arrived.'

'But we're living on our nerves here. All of us. And that's my fault,' she whispered. She was getting upset. 'I've brought all this here and that's not fair. So if TJ knows me and Sam have moved away, you and Mum can live here in peace and not have to keep looking over your shoulders.'

'No. No way,' I said firmly. 'You and Sam can't go on the run from that scumbag. You're safer here where I can protect you. Where would you go?'

She didn't respond for a few seconds. 'But TJ isn't going to go away while we're here. What are you going to do, Dad, kill him?'

'That's not the worst idea, is it?'

Caitlin's eyes widened. 'You shouldn't say stuff like that if you don't mean it.'

I drained the last of my whiskey and took a breath. 'I do mean it. The world would be a better place if he wasn't in it. I'm afraid that's just how I feel.'

Chapter 38

Annie handed Meredith a glass of Prosecco and sat down next to her. They were sitting in the small living room of her flat. Ethan was busy next door doing some of his online work for a law firm.

'Cheers,' Annie said as they clinked glasses. 'Are you allowed to drink alcohol?'

Meredith laughed. 'Oh God, don't try to take that away from me, and yes. Not when I'm having my bloody chemo, but I can when I'm not.'

'Great,' Annie said.

Meredith turned and gave Annie a meaningful look. 'I've been doing a bit of soul searching recently ... since I've had cancer and now that it's a new year.'

Annie arched her brows. 'I'm not discussing your bucket list, if that's what you mean.'

'Oh, I've got a second place to visit if the Taj Mahal doesn't work out.'

'Right, and where's that?' Annie asked. 'Not that we're talking about it though.'

Meredith giggled. 'No, obviously. Weekend in Rhyl.'

Annie rolled her eyes. 'Ha ha. Why has everyone got it in for Rhyl these days? We had some lovely family holidays in Rhyl as a kid.'

'Yeah, well that was before the war, Mum. Long time ago,' Meredith quipped.

'Before the war? You cheeky sod!'

'Anyway, first reserve is Uluru.'

Annie smirked. 'Same to you.'

Meredith laughed. 'Yeah, to a boomer like you, it's called Ayers Rock.'

'I know. I was just messing with you.'

'So that's second, and there's something else that's way more important than any of that.'

Annie gave her a quizzical look. She could tell the tone of the conversation was about to change.

Meredith's voice dropped to a whisper. 'I want to tell Ethan who you are.'

'Really? Why?' Annie had always wanted Ethan to know that she was his grandmother, but Meredith had such misgivings about it that he was still in the dark.

'When I first contacted you,' she explained, 'I just wanted it to be about me and you. You know, me getting to know you as my mum. And Ethan had been through so much with his father leaving, and getting into trouble at school. I just wanted to protect him. The longer he didn't know, the more difficult it felt to tell him. But he deserves to know, and after everything you've been through, you deserve to call him your grandson.'

Annie felt the emotion overwhelm her as tears came into her eyes. She turned and hugged Meredith. 'Yes, I'd really like that. Thank you,' she whispered. 'How do you think he'll take it?'

Chapter 39

It was dawn as Annie and I made our way towards the outskirts of Llangollen where the registered offices of Valley Security were located. I wasn't naïve enough to go in there and confront Terry Palmer and his associate about why they had tried to run us off the road. Annie and I would almost certainly end up in a hole in the middle of Snowdonia, never to be seen again. But what I did want to do is gauge the operation at Valley Security and get a feeling for what we were dealing with. The more information we had, the better. We had also agreed that we'd contact Kelly again, tell her that we'd almost been run off the road by the same Range Rover, and allow her to bring in senior officers from North Wales Police. I wasn't sure what that would lead to, but at my age I just wasn't capable of taking on men like Palmer and those he employed.

Following the satnav, we soon found the bumpy track that led down to a small compound. A sign read *VALLEY SECURITY – Private Property – KEEP OUT! – Trespassers will be prosecuted*. There was also a bright yellow sign with a picture of a black German Shepherd that read *DANGER – Guard Dogs on Patrol.*

The compound was surrounded by towering conifer trees. Since my time working as a ranger in Eryri National Park, I'd become a bit of an expert on the local trees and vegetation. The trees looked like a mixture of Douglas firs and Dutch pines. Even though the snow had mainly thawed overnight, there was still a decent amount on the higher branches of the trees and on the ground below.

The offices comprised of three prefabricated single-storey buildings which had reinforced wire windows. There were four huge tree trunks that had been laid down to form the boundaries of the car park. Most of the compound was also enclosed by a wire fence that must have been 35 to 40 feet high. Dotted around the fence and the prefabs were several security cameras.

'Looks deserted to me,' Annie whispered.

'Yeah. That was what I was counting on,' I whispered back.

She frowned at me. 'Why are we whispering?'

'I don't know.' I smiled. 'You started it.'

She gave me a playful hit on the arm and rolled her eyes.

Opening the door, I got out of the truck. I'd parked just at the entrance of the car park.

The wind picked up, and the leaves and branches shook noisily. I could smell the scent of the pine needles.

Annie gestured over to the cameras that pointed down at us from thick steel fence poles. 'You do know that those security cameras will pick us up?'

'Don't worry, it's just a little sign that we're happy to fuck with them. I don't want them to think we're scared.'

Annie's eyes widened. 'To be honest, Frank, I am scared.'

'Game of bluff, that's all,' I said, trying to reassure her.

Before I could continue, I heard a sound.

A car engine. Or maybe two.

Shit!

I jumped back into the truck and started the ignition. Despite the damage their Range Rover had done to the back of it, there had been nothing structural or mechanical.

I slammed the truck into reverse, but the track to the main road was very narrow. And if it was Palmer, I didn't want to meet him coming the other way.

Glancing left, I saw a small track on the other side of the fence that led into the cover of the trees.

Hitting the accelerator, I turned the truck on full lock and sped down the track. Within a couple of seconds, we were in the darkness of the forest.

I turned off the engine and got out. Annie followed.

'I thought we were just coming to recce the place?' Annie asked, and then shook her head. 'Listen to me. *Recce the place*. I sound like I'm in an episode of some TV cop drama.'

Before I could respond, the sound of car engines grew louder.

Moving slowly behind a tree, I scoured the entrance to the compound and the car park.

Palmer's black Range Rover Sport pulled in at speed and then parked over on the far side closest to the offices.

A black Jaguar F Pace 4x4 pulled in and parked beside it.

The doors to the Range Rover opened. Harris got out of the passenger side and met Palmer at the front of the car.

A figure I recognised got out of the Jaguar.

Andrew Peterman, the MOD lawyer.

Even though it wasn't a huge surprise, I still found myself shocked as I shared a look with Annie.

I took out my phone and took photographs as Palmer and Peterman shook hands.

Got you!

It was time to take all this to the police and let them handle it from here.

Chapter 40

An hour later, I was standing at the paddock of Jones Equestrian Centre and Stables just outside Bala. The air was thick with the earthy, dusty smell of stables – hay, manure, woodchip and leather. There wasn't another smell like it as far as I was concerned.

Annie was nearby on the phone to Kelly. Even though I hated to admit it, once I'd seen Peterman shaking hands with Palmer, I knew we were out of our depth.

Annie ended the call and walked over. 'Meeting at 9am at St Asaph Police Station. Superintendent Gareth Watkins at Dolgellau has contacted the Chief Constable of North Wales Police. He wants to talk to us as soon as possible.'

I gave a little whistle. 'The Chief Constable?' Wheeling out the big guns.' I looked at Annie with a smirk. 'You know the best thing about all this?'

'I do,' she replied with a perceptive expression. 'You're over the moon because DCI Dewi Humphries failed to listen to your concerns about Marcus' suicide even though you told him and Kelly that you thought it was suspicious.'

'Exactly.' I gave a satisfied laugh. 'Given the IOPC are

already investigating that moron for historic failure to do his job properly, he might well be out of a job by the spring. And the thought of that makes me very happy.'

Annie narrowed her eyes. 'I never had you down as a fan of schadenfreude.'

'Bless you,' I joked. I knew that *schadenfreude* was the German for taking pleasure in someone else's failure or suffering.

Annie rolled her eyes. 'Very funny.'

'Anyway, it's not bloody schadenfreude. It's karma,' I pointed out. 'If Dewi did his job properly and wasn't such an arrogant arsehole, Marcus' death would have been investigated properly from the get-go.'

Annie nodded. 'I hear you.' Then she pointed to the chestnut-coloured horse that was being led around the paddock. 'What exactly are we looking at?'

'We're looking at Caitlin's belated Christmas present,' I replied.

'That's very generous.' She sighed dramatically. 'All I got was a scarf.'

'A bloody Hermes scarf, thank you,' I joked. 'Sam loves riding and so does Caitlin. She needs a horse so she can go out with him when I'm not around.'

'And this is a good horse then?'

'Morgan filly. Three years old. A good versatile breed, and gentle. Perfect for Caitlin as she can be a bit of a nervous rider.

'She's beautiful.'

'Yes, she is,' I said.

For a few minutes, we just watched various horses being walked around.

Just as I prepared myself to arrange delivery of Caitlin's horse, I saw something out of the corner of my eye.

The sunlight reflecting off the windscreen of a fast-approaching car.

Turning slowly, I squinted and saw the car parking.

It was Palmer's Range Rover.

And he'd boxed my truck in.

My heart started to pound. 'Shit!' I said under my breath.

Annie turned and saw it too. 'How the hell did they know we were here?'

'They must have put a tracker on my truck,' I said angrily. 'I should have checked.'

My mind was whirring.

How are we going to get out of this?

We couldn't leave in my truck.

And we couldn't outrun them.

My eyes scanned the paddock and stables.

'What are we going to do?' Annie asked, sounding nervous.

'I'm working on it.'

I glanced back. The doors to the Range Rover opened and Palmer and Harris got out. They were both wearing sunglasses and black baseball caps.

I saw Palmer tap his coat on his chest just below his armpit.

I knew what that meant.

He was armed and had a handgun in a shoulder holster.

This is really bad.

I put my hand on Annie's shoulder and looked at her.

'We're going over this fence into the paddock,' I said, as my brain worked out the best means of escape.

'Why?' Her eyes widened with fear as she saw the two men approaching.

I grabbed her hand. 'Just trust me,' I snapped.

I stepped up onto the rough wooden poles of the paddock's fence.

Reaching down, I pulled Annie as she climbed up.

I threw my leg over the top, and helped her do the same.

I jumped down onto the woodchips and earth on the other side. Putting my hands up, I took Annie's weight and lowered her down.

I took her hand. 'Come on.'

We sprinted over to the chestnut-coloured horse that we'd been watching.

One of the men who worked at the paddock approached. 'Everything okay, Frank?'

'Yeah.' I put my foot into the stirrup. 'I'll take her right now.'

The man looked baffled. 'Now?'

'Long story,' I said as I got up and into the saddle.

'What am I going to do?' Annie asked, looking up at me.

'You're coming with me.' I reached down and took her hand. 'Put your foot here, on top of mine.'

'Are you kidding me?'

'No.'

I grabbed her by the forearm and pulled her as she pushed up on my foot that was in the stirrup.

Lifting her, I grabbed her coat as she twisted onto the saddle behind me.

'I can't believe we're doing this,' she muttered.

I kicked my heels against the horse's sides. 'I don't think we have a choice. Palmer is armed.'

The horse shot away as I looped my hands around the reins.

Annie squealed, and wrapped her arms around my waist tightly.

Several of the onlookers looked confused as we cantered across the paddock towards the closed gate.

Glancing back, I saw Palmer and Harris look at each other, turn, and start to run back towards the Range Rover.

I gave the horse another dig with my heels. 'Come on, girl,' I said as we sped towards the gate. 'Hold right on, Annie!' I yelled.

Using the reins, the horse sailed over the gate and we landed on the other side.

Thank God!

Looking out to our right, I saw the countryside stretching away for as far as the eye could see.

'Come on,' I said again with encouragement.

The sound of the hooves thundering against the moorland was loud and rhythmic.

'Where are we going?' Annie shouted above the noise.

'No idea yet, but I've been riding this area since I was a boy.'

The cold wind swirled around us.

As we galloped away, clumps of mud flew into the air behind us.

Then I became aware of another sound.

A car engine.

Glancing back, I saw that the Range Rover was hammering across the fields behind us.

Shit!

Part of me had hoped that they wouldn't pursue us cross-country.

'Frank!' Annie shouted in a worried voice.

'I know,' I yelled. 'I've seen them.'

Even at top speed, the horse wasn't going to go more than 30mph. And the terrain was wet and uneven, so probably less.

I stood up on the stirrups for a second and looked to our left.

There was the deep roar of the Range Rover's 4.4 litre V8 engine.

Then the car appeared and drew level with us.

Palmer looked across at me. He signalled for me to stop, as if it was futile for us to try and outrun him. But I wasn't going to stop. We were in the middle of nowhere and I had no idea what they intended to do to us.

I started to form a plan in my head.

I gave Palmer a grin and a little wave. *Piss off, dickhead.*

Then I pulled the reins hard left, looped back behind the car, and cut towards the Carneddau mountains which loomed up in the distance.

However, a few seconds later, it was behind us again. And then with a loud rev of its engine, it was parallel to us, this time to our right.

There was no way we were going to outrun them.

Glancing right, I saw Harris looking at me and shaking his head.

Oh fuck off, will you.

Then the car swerved towards us.

I had to pull the horse violently to the left and try to slow her down.

They were going to drive into us and knock the horse over and us with it.

'We need to stop!' Annie shouted.

'No!' I yelled, as I spotted what I was looking for.

Llewelyn's Clogwyn. Or Llewelyn's Bluff.

It was about two hundred yards ahead of us.

That's if we made it.

I hadn't been here for decades.

But if I remembered correctly, *Llewelyn's Clogwyn* was a

hundred-foot precipice that seemed to come from nowhere.

At its bottom, there were huge boulders and broken rocks that I'd played on as a boy.

It was the only thing I could think of.

And it was incredibly dangerous and risky.

Repeating the same manoeuvre, I slowed the horse and looped back behind the car to buy some time.

It worked, and Palmer had to adjust the position of his car again.

100 yards to go.

'Frank!' Annie yelled.

'Just hold on!' I shouted back.

I looked ahead, willing us to get to *Llewelyn's Clogwyn* before we were smashed off the horse and killed.

The car pulled up beside us again.

50 yards.

It swerved towards us.

Shit!

Glancing down, I saw the side of it actually clip my right foot by a fraction.

'Woah,' I slowed the horse again.

20 yards.

I looked ahead. This was it.

Even though it was almost completely invisible, the edge of the bluff was coming towards us at speed.

If the horse was as well trained as I thought she was, I could stop her in one to two seconds.

But the Range Rover would take longer. And the ground was icy and wet.

10 yards.

I glanced over at Palmer again.

I gave him a wink. I couldn't help myself.

'HOLD ON!' I yelled at the top of my voice. Then I pulled the reins and thundered, 'WOAH! WOAH, GIRL!'

I held my breath.

Please God, let this work.

The horse reared a little and used her back legs to stop almost immediately.

Palmer was still looking over at me.

Then he saw the precipice.

It was too late.

He slammed on the brakes.

The car skidded for the final five yards across the wet ground.

Then it tipped over the side of the bluff and vanished.

'Jesus Christ!' I turned and looked at Annie who was white. 'Are you okay?'

She nodded but didn't speak.

Standing up on the stirrups, I did a jumping dismount. I didn't care. I was full of adrenaline so couldn't feel a thing.

Racing to the edge of the bluff, I saw that the Range Rover had fallen and then rolled to the bottom.

It was now on its roof.

Annie jumped down and came to my side. 'Jesus, Frank. If that was your plan, then you're a bloody genius,' she gasped.

I wasn't convinced we were out of the woods quite yet.

'They can't have survived that, can they?' she whispered.

To my horror, I watched as both the passenger door and the driver's door opened slowly.

'You've got to be joking, haven't you?' I groaned.

At first, the doors just lay there open.

Then we watched as, very slowly, Palmer and Harris crawled out on their hands and knees.

Even from here, I could see their faces were covered in blood.

It looked like our nightmare still wasn't over.

Annie looked at me and shook her head. I could see how frightened she was.

Suddenly, there was a huge BANG.

I jumped out of my skin.

The Range Rover was engulfed in a huge ball of orange flames as the petrol tank exploded.

A colossal cloud of black smoke rose into the air.

After a few seconds, the flames and smoke died down a little.

I could see the blackened bodies of the two men lying motionless on the ground.

Chapter 41

An hour later, Annie and I were sitting in the car park at the stables. There were three police patrol cars and a fire engine in attendance. Paramedics and a forensics team were down at the crash site.

Annie had a red blanket draped around her shoulders. She was still trembling, and the paramedics were worried that she was in shock. A young female paramedic finished taking her blood pressure and unfastened the inflatable arm cuff.

'How am I?' Annie asked as she sipped her sweet tea.

'Blood pressure is up a bit. So is your pulse,' came the reply, but then she raised an eyebrow. 'Given what I've been told you've just been through, I'd say you're doing pretty well.'

I smiled. 'Yeah, despite the accent and clothes, Annie's a tough old bird.'

'Oi,' Annie laughed, giving me a dig in the ribs for good measure.

The paramedic looked at Annie. 'Your husband must

be a hell of a horse rider. I hear you were being chased by some guys in a Range Rover.'

'I'm not her husband,' I corrected her quietly. In recent months, Annie and I had spent increasing amounts of time together, but she was my best friend. We had the same sense of humour and view of the world – well, most of the time - but it was no more than that. And while Rachel was alive, it was never going to be. When Rachel did finally pass, I had no idea what would happen between us. I didn't want that thought to enter my mind. It felt duplicitous to even give it space in my head at the moment.

'Oh, sorry,' she apologised. 'I just assumed …'

'No. He's definitely not my husband, thank God,' Annie chortled, 'but he's a very dear friend.'

I looked up and saw Kelly approaching. She had a slightly bewildered expression on her face.

'How are you guys doing?' she asked with a concerned expression.

'Okay, I think,' I said with a shrug.

'Good, good.' She nodded, deep in thought. 'If you're up to it, we'd like you to come to St Asaph later?'

I looked at Annie.

'Or we can do it tomorrow?' Kelly suggested.

'No.' Annie shook her head. 'I'm fine. Let's get it done today.'

IT WAS LATE AFTERNOON. The large meeting room had a light-coloured oval table and about ten chairs around it. Annie and I had been describing all that had happened in recent days, and our cross-country chase a few hours ago. Tony Bridgestock, the Chief Constable of North Wales Police

– and therefore the highest-ranking officer in the region – had led on the meeting. There had been no suggestion that Annie and I were culpable of anything. Kelly sat opposite us, making copious amounts of notes on her electronic notepad. Dewi was conspicuous by his absence, given that not only was he a DCI, but he had attended the scene of Marcus' death. I wondered if I should enquire about his whereabouts, given that he had chosen to ignore my concerns at the scene.

Bridgestock was one of the new breed of police officers in the force. A fast-tracked graduate who was more politician than 'copper'. But I had nothing against him, and I'd seen plenty of decent coppers make a right balls-up when they reached the upper echelons of the force. Either the power and status went to their heads and they became pompous mini dictators, or they became frozen by the fear of making the big decisions and were completely ineffectual.

'I've spoken to the forensics team down at the scene,' Bridgestock explained. 'Although there will be a postmortem, there's no reason to believe that Terry Palmer and Ashley Harris were killed by anything other than the car explosion.' Then he gave me a considered look. Everything he'd done since he walked in the room had been considered. 'I know that you and Annie have your own theories about why these men were following you in recent days and why they chased you today.'

I frowned. 'They're not theories,' I said firmly.

Bridgestock ignored me. 'There will be a full investigation. And we have already referred ourselves to the IOPC for investigation, as I'm aware that CID officers at the scene of Marcus Daniels' death failed to take your legitimate concerns seriously. Although we've never worked together, I know you by reputation Frank. It was remiss of our officers not to take what you suspected with the gravity and importance that it deserved.'

Annie leaned forward. 'There must be evidence at the premises of Valley Security that will connect Palmer and Harris to Marcus' death. Laptops, phone records?'

Kelly raised her head and looked across at us. 'I'm afraid that the premises of Valley Security, and everything in it, were destroyed by fire this afternoon.'

'What?' I snapped angrily as I got out my phone. 'I've got photographs of Palmer and Harris meeting Andrew Peterman at those premises. Peterman is a Ministry of Defence lawyer for God's sake. You need to ask him what he was doing there!' I felt myself beginning to lose my temper. I could see how this was going to go. Another whitewash. Another cover-up.

Bridgestock raised his shoulders. 'We will, of course, be interviewing Andrew Peterman, but he hasn't broken any law by meeting these two men. And if we can't find anything linking Palmer and Harris to Marcus Daniels or his death we don't have anything to go on.' He looked at me again. 'Sorry, Frank. I know what you saw when you found Marcus was suspicious but it's all circumstantial.'

I shook my head in bewilderment, and felt Annie stiffen beside me. 'What are you trying to say?' she said abruptly. 'That you're not going investigate Marcus' death because you have no evidence? Isn't it your job to <u>find</u> the evidence?'

'Let me reassure both of you that we will do everything in our power to find out who killed Marcus and bring them to justice. That's if he was indeed murdered,' Bridgestock said in his well-rehearsed sincere voice that wasn't fooling me. 'I just want to sound a note of caution that we may never find out if Marcus was killed, why, or by who.'

Chapter 42

Annie came into Richard Daniels' living room with a tray. It was late afternoon now and dark outside. We had agreed that we should visit Richard after the events of the day.

'Here we go,' Annie said, as she set the tray down on a small coffee table. 'Richard, I've borrowed your lovely teapot. And there were some loose Assam tea leaves so I used those.'

The teapot had a beautifully intricate pattern of dark reds and gold.

'Perfect,' Richard said with a half smile. 'Both are legacies of my late wife's Indian heritage. She would have definitely approved. It was a bit of a bug bear of hers that I preferred Yorkshire tea to any other in the world.'

'I'm with you there, Richard,' I said in agreement as Annie poured the tea into delicate china teacups through an old-fashioned metal strainer.

He leaned forward with very shaky hands. 'Very civilised though.' He took the cup with both hands to steady it. 'Bloody hell,' he grumbled under his breath.

Then he took a sip and placed the cup carefully down on the table. I could see how much his Parkinson's was affecting him, and how much effort it was taking for him just to do something as simple as drink tea.

'Sugar?' Annie asked me.

'Please. Two.' I watched as she used a tiny silver spoon to take the sugar from a bowl.

Richard sat back and gave us both a meaningful look. 'I can't thank you enough for everything you've done. You've both risked your lives to find out what happened to Marcus.'

'Oh, we haven't finished quite yet, Richard,' Annie reassured him.

He looked puzzled. 'Haven't you?'

'No. We know the two men who killed your son,' she announced, 'and they're dead now.'

A shadow of pain flickered across his brow. 'I'm not proud to admit it, but I'm glad they're dead. Marcus and I didn't always see eye to eye on everything, but he was my son and I loved him. I don't think I could have coped with sitting through a trial.'

'No,' I agreed. 'That would have been very difficult.'

'I'm determined to find out who gave the orders for Marcus to be killed,' Annie said firmly, 'and I've put out some feelers already.'

'Right,' he said, looking quickly at me before continuing. 'If you have the strength and inclination to take on the Ministry of Defence, then good luck to you both.'

As I sat forward to take my cup of tea from my saucer and give it a stir, I glanced around the room and spotted something very high up on a bookshelf.

An empty bottle of Moet & Chandon Champagne. Beside it were two Champagne flutes. I wasn't sure if it was significant or not, but they were at a height which Richard couldn't reach now with Parkinson's. It would be a stretch to put them up there even if he was fully fit. Maybe they had been there for years and were covered with dust. Frankly, I wasn't sure why I was giving this any thought. It wasn't my business.

'I've reached out to one of the investigative journalists that I've got to know over the years,' Annie explained. 'A lovely woman called Molly Ferguson who works for the investigative team at The Sunday Times. I've given her a few broad notes, but clearly I don't want to say too much until we meet. I really do think it's important that we get full justice for Marcus.'

Richard nodded in agreement. 'Do you know much about the men who … killed him?'

Taking out my phone, I selected one of the photos that I'd taken earlier that morning at the Valley Security compound. I zoomed in a little, and then went and crouched beside Richard to show him.

'This is a photograph that I took this morning,' I said as I showed Richard the phone screen. 'This man is Terry Palmer, and this is Ashley Harris. They are ex-SAS mercenaries. They run a private security firm, Valley Security. This other man is Andrew Peterman. He's an MOD lawyer. We think that Peterman hired Palmer and Harris to kill Marcus.'

For a few seconds, Richard just stared at the photograph. He was full of emotion, and his bottom lip trembled as if he was about to cry.

'I see,' he whispered.

I put a reassuring hand on his shoulder. 'I'm so sorry.'

I put the phone down on the coffee table and went and sat down.

Then he looked at Annie. 'And this was an MOD directive?'

She shook her head. 'That's what I don't know, and it's what I'm determined to find out.'

Chapter 43

As we drove away from Richard's home, I glanced up at the clear evening sky and noticed that the moon was rising over to our left. A sprinkling of silver stars were becoming sharper in focus in the blackness, and the line of mountains to our left had completely disappeared. They might reappear once the moon was at its peak in the sky.

I was tired, and I needed some music to soothe me. I reached into my pocket for my phone, and realised that it wasn't there.

Where the hell is my phone? I wondered. Then I remembered. I'd put it on the coffee table when I'd shown Richard the photos from the Valley Security compound.

'Bugger,' I said under my breath as I applied the brakes gently. 'I've left my phone on Richard's coffee table.'

'It's less than ten minutes back there,' Annie reassured me as she was reading on her own phone.

I made a careful U-turn and headed back.

'Email from that journalist I was telling you about,' she said, gesturing to her phone. 'Molly Ferguson. She's going to travel up here the day after tomorrow to see what we've got.'

'Great.' I was determined not to let Peterman and anyone else involved in Marcus' death get away with it.

'Do you remember the 'cash for questions' scandal in the 1990s?' Annie asked.

'Yes, vaguely. Remind me.'

'Molly was working for The Guardian at the time. She discovered that Ian Greer, the most powerful and influential Parliamentary lobbyist in the country, had bribed two Conservative MPs to ask questions in the House of Commons for Mohamed Al-Fayed.'

'It's all coming back to me. That was her?'

'Yes. She definitely knows her stuff and she doesn't take any prisoners.'

'Sounds ideal for us then,' I said as I turned into Richard's road.

There was a car parked outside where I'd been parked only ten minutes before. A Land Rover Defender, which I knew from somewhere but couldn't place.

Annie gestured to the car. 'Richard's got visitors. Maybe they were waiting for us to go?' she joked.

For some reason, I slowed the truck and parked a little bit down the road from the house. I don't know what it was. In the old days they called it my 'copper's nose'. I got a feeling that something wasn't quite right. I didn't know why or what.

'I'm just going to pop and get my phone,' I said nonchalantly. I wasn't quite sure how to articulate how I was feeling, and now wasn't the time to explore it. 'Back in a minute.'

Jumping out of the truck into the darkness, I made my way along the grassy verge that acted as a pathway along the front of the houses in the road.

Looking at the Land Rover Defender, I realised where I knew it from.

It belonged to Owen, Sian's brother.

Nothing suspicious in that, was there? Maybe Richard had called Owen to tell him about our visit. I guessed that Kelly and other members of the North Wales Police would have visited Sian that afternoon to tell her about the accident involving us, as well as Palmer and Harris' deaths.

As I reached the edge of the driveway, I saw a figure coming out of the house carrying two heavy-looking suitcases.

As the figure came into the light, I saw that it was Richard!

He was straight-backed, walking quite normally, and there was no shaking.

What the hell is going on? I wondered, as I moved back very slowly and used the tall hedge as cover.

Richard unlocked the Land Rover, opened up the hatch at the back, and then heaved up the suitcases into the boot area.

Are you bloody joking?

Either he had received a miracle cure in the past ten minutes, or he'd been faking his Parkinson's disease all along.

You lying fucker!

I couldn't believe my eyes. Why had he deceived us? Had he kept up that act with everyone? I assumed that he'd also been faking his Parkinson's when dealing with the police.

But why?

Another figure came out of the house, but before I could get a clear look they went back inside.

That had to be Owen, didn't it?

'Don't forget your wellies,' Richard called back to

whoever was in the house. Then I saw him take out his phone and stare down at it. The light from the screen lit up his face.

I'd gladly go over there and beat him to a bloody pulp for what he'd done. But I still didn't understand why.

'I think we should head off at midnight,' he said, looking down at his phone.

Whoever was inside the house didn't respond.

The clouds moved slowly up in the sky to reveal the moon which bathed everything in a soft, vanilla glow.

Richard suddenly looked in my direction and peered into the darkness.

I took a step back and my boot made a noise on some gravel.

'Hello?' he called out. 'Is anyone there?'

I froze.

'Hello?' he called again, and took a step forward.

A dog started to bark from somewhere in the distance.

The wind picked up and the bushes and trees all around shook and rattled.

A clump of snow from a branch high above fell and landed on the back of my neck. It fell down my jacket and onto my skin.

Jesus, that's freezing!

I knew that I couldn't move or make a sound.

The figure from the house appeared again.

'So kind of my brother to lend us his car,' said a woman's voice that I recognised.

It was Sian Daniels.

'We're going to need it if we're going to the Highlands this time of year,' Richard said.

Sian was carrying a pair of green wellies.

'Here, give those to me,' Richard said in an over-friendly tone as he took the wellies from her and put them into the Land Rover.

Bloody hell, Sian is in on this too? What the …?

Richard slammed the hatch shut. Then he took Sian in his arms and they kissed passionately.

Fuck me! Now I've seen everything, I thought.

Richard and Sian are having an affair? His own bloody daughter-in-law? That's disgusting. How could he do that to Marcus?

I watched in amazement as they walked arm and arm back into the house and closed the front door.

My phone! I need to get my bloody phone. I can't leave it in there.

Walking as casually as I could down the drive, I could feel my pulse racing. I still couldn't get my head around what I'd seen. Did that mean they'd plotted to kill Marcus? Had Annie and I got it completely wrong?

I knocked hesitantly on the front door.

Silence.

I knew that Richard and Sian would be thrown by my appearance, but I wasn't about to confront them with what I'd seen. I needed to talk to Annie and make a plan first.

The door opened very slowly, and Sian looked out at me. She'd gone from appearing bright and breezy in Richard's company, to looking haunted and grief-stricken in a matter of seconds.

You devious cow.

'Hi Sian …'

'Looking for this?' she asked very quietly as she handed me my phone. 'Richard said that you'd left it here by accident.'

'How's he doing?' I asked with fake concern. It was clear that he was doing a lot better than I could have ever expected.

She gave me a weary look. 'We've both been through

so much. The police and Richard told me what you did today. I can't thank you enough.'

'It's fine,' I reassured her through gritted teeth. 'Well, thanks for the phone. I'll let you get on.'

She gave me a thankful nod as she closed the door.

Unbelievable.

I walked slowly up the driveway and along to my truck. My head was whirring with thoughts.

I opened the driver's door and sat down in utter shock.

'Got your phone?' Annie asked.

'What? Erm, yes,' I whispered.

She looked at me through narrowed eyes. 'God, you look like you've seen a ghost.'

'Well, I have. Sort of,' I said with a puzzled expression.

'What do you mean?'

I gave her a dark look. 'Richard doesn't have Parkinson's for starters.

'What? Are you sure?'

'Yes. Certain. He's also having an affair with Sian Daniels,' I said quietly.

'What? Have you taken drugs?' she asked accusingly.

'No,' I took a breath, 'and I'm pretty sure that Richard and Sian murdered Marcus.'

Chapter 44

Annie and I sat at her kitchen table, still trying to take in what I'd seen at Richard's home. I was now nursing a large glass of whiskey in my hand. I needed to take the edge off.

'You're right.' Annie looked at me as she took a sip of her red wine. 'They have to have murdered Marcus. There's no other possible explanation about why they've both been lying to us. Or why Richard faked having Parkinson's.'

'No, but why kill Marcus?' I shook my head. 'Clearly, it's unforgivable for Richard and Sian to be having an affair, but they could have come clean and got on with their lives. And Marcus with his.'

'Life insurance and Marcus' army pension?' Annie suggested. Then she frowned. 'I just need to check something.' She took her phone and started to tap on it.

'What are you looking for?'

'I'm searching LinkedIn,' she said, looking distracted.

'I don't know that is,' I admitted.

She pointed to the screen and then gave me a meaningful look. 'I've found Sian Daniels on it. I can't believe that we never looked before.'

'Why? What is it?'

'She's a practice nurse with over twenty-five years' experience.'

'So, she knows how to use a syringe ... and how to inject someone directly into the carotid artery,' I said, slowly thinking out loud.

Annie sighed. 'None of this is going to be enough to convict them though, is it?'

'No,' I replied with frustration.

My phone rang. It was Kelly. I'd left her a voicemail telling her to contact us as it was urgent.

'Frank?' Kelly said as I answered. 'I got your message. Are you and Annie okay?'

'Yes, we're fine,' I reassured her.

'That's a relief. I'm sitting looking at something that digital forensics have found, and I can't seem to make head nor tail of it.'

'Nothing you can tell me tonight is going to surprise me,' I said wearily, 'but go on.' I wanted to see if what she had found tallied with what we'd discovered about Richard and Sian.

'You sent me that video from Tinsdale's doorbell camera. The one that had Terry Palmer's Range Rover on it?'

'That's right. There was a car out of focus with its headlights on over by Marcus' drive.'

'The tech boys have managed to clean up that image. We've got a clear look at the licence plate, but it doesn't make sense,' she said, sounding puzzled.

'Why not?'

'The car is registered to Richard Daniels, but he has severe Parkinson's so he can't drive. And he's never made any mention that he or someone driving his car was at Marcus' home on New Year's Eve.'

'Richard Daniels doesn't have Parkinson's,' I said matter-of-factly.

'What?' Kelly spluttered.

'He doesn't have Parkinson's, and he's having an affair with Sian Daniels. We're convinced that they killed Marcus. We just don't think there's enough evidence to charge them.'

'Erm … I'm totally confused now, Frank,' Kelly admitted.

I began to recount what I'd seen earlier that evening.

Chapter 45

Annie and I shared a look as I knocked on Richard Daniels' door at 11.15pm. We were in plenty of time, as I knew that he and Sian were heading to Scotland at midnight.

My breath froze in the icy air as we waited on the doorstep.

Silence.

I let out a frustrated sigh. I knew they were in.

Finally, there was the sound of the front door being unlocked.

The door opened very slowly and Richard peered out.

'Frank?' he asked, acting as if he'd been asleep. He stood with his back crooked, leg bouncing a little, and his hand that held the door shaking.

I fixed him with an angry stare. 'You can cut out all the Parkinson's bollocks for starters, Richard. I know you've been faking it.'

Silence. Richard blinked as he took in what I'd said to him.

'Faking it?' He looked horrified. 'What are you talking about, Frank? Have you been drinking?'

I took an aggressive step forward as my nostrils flared. My patience was wearing thin. 'Either you stop the whole act or I'll give you something to really shake about.'

He took a few seconds to weigh up his options. Then, as if by magic, his shaking stopped, he stood up straight, and he took a deep breath.

'Almost biblical, isn't it?' Annie said sardonically.

I took another step towards him and the door. 'I think you need to let us in.'

'Can I stop you?' he asked.

'No,' I snapped angrily as I went inside with Annie behind me. 'Where's Sian?'

Before he had time to respond, Sian appeared at the top of the stairs. 'What is it, Richard? What's going on down there?'

'I'm going to need you to come down here right now, Sian,' I said in a tone that left no doubt that I meant business.

'Frank? What are you doing here?' she said in a tone that told me she was still playing the part of a grieving widow.

Richard looked up at her. Sian noticed that his fake Parkinson's symptoms had disappeared.

'I don't know what all this is about, Sian, but you need to come down,' he said solemnly. 'Frank wants to talk to us.'

'In there!' I growled as I pointed to the living room door.

Richard and Sian scuttled in.

'Sit down there,' I barked as they sat down on the sofa.

Annie and I then sat down on the two seats opposite.

Richard gave me a supercilious look. 'I have no idea

what all this is about, Frank, but I'm sure we can work it all out in a civilised manner.' He was definitely rattled.

Annie narrowed her eyes. 'Is this the same *civilised manner* that you adopted when you murdered your own son and then faked his suicide?'

Silence. You could have heard a pin drop.

The blood visibly drained from Sian's face.

I glared at her. 'We know that you injected Marcus with a sedative that you probably took from the surgery where you work. Something that wouldn't show up in a toxicology report. You're a nurse, so you have access to syringes and heavy tranquillisers.'

'No. Why are you saying that?' She shook her head. 'You've got it all wrong!'

'Really?' Annie gave her a withering look. 'You both need to stop lying. We've got video of Richard's car parked at the top of your drive about ten minutes before Marcus was killed.'

Richard gave a nonchalant shrug. 'I haven't committed a crime by being there.'

I glared directly at him, wondering how I'd managed to get it so wrong. 'Come on, Richard!' I snapped loudly. 'Don't lie to us. We know you and Sian are having an affair. We know that Sian drugged Marcus and that you drove over to help her stage his suicide.'

Richard laughed. 'God, Frank. That's a hell of a theory.'

'It's not a theory,' I said firmly, shaking my head.

Annie turned to Sian. 'You need to stop lying, Sian. We know that's what happened.'

Sian dissolved into tears. 'Wait. You don't understand. You don't understand what Marcus was like.'

Richard gave me a cold, icy stare. 'What do you want, Frank? You know that you can't prove that Sian and I murdered Marcus in a court of law. You haven't got any evidence. Nothing that the CPS would ever go to trial over.'

I fixed him with a malevolent gaze. 'He was your son, Richard. How could you do that to your own son?'

'He was no son of mine,' he spat. 'We hated each other. We always had done. Marcus had a string of affairs. Poor Sian kept giving him chance after chance. I guess I was just a shoulder to cry on. One thing led to another.'

'That's not a reason to kill him!' Annie exclaimed.

Sian lifted her phone as she wiped the tears from her face. 'I found photos of Marcus and that girl from his school.' She turned the phone to show a photo of Marcus having sex with Layla O'Dowd. It was explicit, and I was slightly shocked. 'She was only seventeen years old! It was disgusting. He should have gone to prison.'

'But he didn't go to prison. You killed him instead,' I said in disbelief.

'Yes,' Richard said with no hint of emotion.

'Marcus had made my life hell for thirty years,' Sian sobbed.

I shrugged. 'You could have just divorced him.'

Silence.

'But if you'd divorced him, you wouldn't get his army pension, would you?' Annie said.

'And if he's dead, you get his life insurance and the house,' I added.

Silence.

Richard ran a palm along his jaw, as if to aid his thinking. 'Okay. Well done, Frank. You've solved it. Marcus went outside for a smoke. I held him and Sian injected him. Then we staged it so that it looked like a suicide.' He gave me a smug smile. 'But you can't prove it.'

'Maybe not. There is one thing though. Why did you

change your will so that Marcus was the sole beneficiary? That doesn't make any sense.'

'Just in case anyone suspected that Sian and I had anything to do with his death. I'd hardly make him the sole beneficiary of my will if I wanted to harm him, would I?'

Annie nodded. 'And of course with Marcus dead, Sian is now the sole beneficiary of your will. But no one is going to ask any awkward questions and you don't have to change it.'

'Precisely.' Richard sighed loudly and stood up. 'Well this is all fascinating, but Sian and I have got travel plans for tonight. And I'm really sorry, Frank, but there isn't a shred of evidence to prove what I've just told you. So, unless you're going to beat us both into writing and signing a confession, I suggest that you leave and let us get on our way.'

I stood up and squared up to Richard. I really had misjudged him over the years. I knew he had the capacity to be arrogant and pompous, but a cold killer of his own son?

'No, Richard,' I said calmly as I went out into the hallway. 'I'm not going to beat a confession out of you. I don't really need to.'

A look of confusion crossed his face as I went to the front door.

'What's he talking about?' Sian asked Richard quietly.

'I'm not sure,' he remarked sourly. 'Some kind of stupid riddle.'

I gave Annie a knowing wink as I opened the door.

Standing on the doorstep was Kelly, along with three burly-looking uniformed police officers.

Opening my jacket and then my shirt, I revealed the small microphone that had been taped to my chest just before we'd knocked on the door.

'Did you get everything you need, Detective Sergeant Thomas?' I asked with a smirk.

'Oh my God,' Sian whimpered.

'Yes. Perfect.' Kelly looked at Richard and Sian. 'Richard Daniels and Sian Daniels, I'm arresting you for the murder of Marcus Daniels. You do not have to say anything, but it may harm your defence if you do not mention, when questioned, something which you later rely on in court.'

Chapter 46

One Week Later

I held up Annie's new front door, taking some of the weight as I tried to line up the final hinge at the bottom. I'd been working on it for nearly two hours and was relatively pleased with the job I'd done. It'd been a few years since I'd sanded and fitted a new door.

Begin Again by *Taylor Swift* started to play. At first, I looked around to see where the music was coming from before remembering that it was now the ringtone on my phone. Caitlin had set it up for me as a little joke between me and Annie – although she'd yet to hear it.

Whoever was calling me would have to wait for a bit. I had my hands full and I needed to finish the door.

The ringtone stopped.

Pushing the drill hard, I squeezed the red 'trigger' and watched with satisfaction as the final screw went into the bottom of the hinge. Then I stood back to admire my handiwork.

Well Frank, that's a pretty good fit.

Annie appeared with the third mug of coffee of the day. 'Here we go. Strong and black.'

'Thank you,' I said as I took the mug from her and had a swig.

She looked at the door and grinned. 'Shall I try it?'

I laughed. 'Give it a test drive.'

She went to the door and closed it.

We stood together for a few seconds just looking at it as if it was some exquisite piece of art.

It was a perfect fit. I'd even fitted draft excluders around the edges.

'Brilliant,' she said in an upbeat tone. 'How the hell do you know how to do all these things?'

I shrugged. 'My old man. He showed me everything when I was a boy. He was a hell of a carpenter. Could make you anything.'

The thought of my father always gave me such ambivalent feelings.

'Complicated relationship, wasn't it?' she said gently. She'd heard me talk about him before.

'Very complicated,' I agreed.

Before I could say anything else, my phone rang again.

On hearing the *Taylor Swift* ringtone, Annie roared with laughter. 'Oh my God, Frank. That is hilarious.'

I smiled at her and then looked at the phone's screen. It was Mel from Jones Equestrian Centre and Stables. The horse that I'd bought for Caitlin was still there, as she needed to have her final injections and a bill of health from the equestrian vet. Then they would deliver her to us.

I looked at Annie who was still sniggering at my ringtone. 'Hi Mel, how can I help?'

'We're not going to be able to deliver your horse until early next week,' she explained. 'Outbreak of BVD over this way so every vet is out dealing with that.'

'Not a problem,' I reassured her. 'Just let me know when you're arriving and I'll make sure I'm there.'

'That's great. Thanks, Frank,' she said as she ended the call.

I held my phone for a second, and noticed that Annie was giving me a knowing look.

She started to chuckle. 'You do know that ringtone now makes you a *Swifty*?'

'I'm going to pretend that I know what that is,' I said dryly.

Chapter 47

That afternoon, Rachel, Caitlin, Sam and I made our way across the graveyard at St Mary's Church in Dolgellau. The church itself was a Grade II listed building built in the 1700s, although there had been a church on the site since 1254.

We walked in silence along the narrow gravel pathway that hugged the east flank of the church. To our left there were uneven lines of graves that dated back centuries. Draped urns and obelisks, lopsided slabs and headstones where the ground had subsided. Thick small-leaved ivy covered a few smaller stones. Over by the far wall an old yew bent sideways, its trunk and leafless branches smoothed by the relentless wind that came in from the mountains.

The crunching of our shoes and boots were rhythmic. Although I hadn't visited it since the funeral, I knew where James' grave was. Just up the central pathway, over to the right, next to my mother and father.

I walked next to Sam, who had his head slightly bowed and seemed deep in thought. He was holding a small bunch of snowdrops for the uncle who he'd never got to meet.

'You okay?' I asked him quietly.

He nodded but didn't speak, as if it wasn't appropriate to talk in this small city of the dead. Maybe he was right.

Caitlin and her mother walked ahead of us, arm in arm. Rachel had been confused about where we were going, although we'd all patiently reminded her several times. Her own parents were buried over in Corwen.

Out of the corner of my eye I spotted my mother's grave and then my father's. They had both died in 2003, within six months of each other. My father had gone first, and I always wondered if my mother had died from a broken heart. She wasn't an emotional woman, but maybe the loss of her husband of half a century just overwhelmed her.

I knew that James' headstone and grave was the next on the right, but for a few seconds I couldn't bring myself to look. I watched as Rachel and Caitlin leaned down over it. Caitlin removed some dead flowers and two small tealight candles that had rusted. I had no idea who had brought them or when.

I gritted my teeth as my eyes went to the headstone, but it was too much. The tears came and I took a deep breath.

'You were right, Frank,' Rachel said, looking up at me from where she was now crouched down. She swept her hand over the headstone as if polishing it. 'It is beautiful.'

I nodded and put my hand to my face. I didn't want to let Sam see me like this.

Caitlin came over and put her arms around me. 'Dad, hey.'

'Sorry,' I whispered, trying to catch my breath. 'I didn't know it was going to affect me like this.'

'Don't apologise,' she said as she took a step back.

I could see Sam looking up at me. I quickly wiped my face and nose and gave him a joyless smile.

'I didn't want Sam to see me like this,' I said quietly to Caitlin.

'Why? It's 2023, Dad. I want Sam to see that it's okay for men to cry and show their emotions. Especially you. You're his role model. I don't want him to ever bottle things up and think that crying or being emotional is a sign of weakness.' She glanced at James' grave. 'Terrible things can happen when you do that.'

I saw that Sam had taken a couple of tentative steps towards me.

'Are you sad, Taid?' he asked softly.

I looked down into his eyes and hooked a finger under his chin, tipping his face towards me. 'Yes, I'm sad Sam. We're all feeling sad. But that's okay, mate.'

ENJOY THIS BOOK?

PREORDER THE NEXT FRANK MARSHAL BOOK NOW

My Book
https://www.amazon.com/dp/B0DZPC15LC

Your FREE book is waiting for you now

Get your FREE copy of the prequel to
the DI Ruth Hunter Series NOW
http://www.simonmccleave.com/vip-email-club
and join my VIP Email Club

DC RUTH HUNTER SERIES

London, 1997. A series of baffling murders. A web of political corruption. DC Ruth Hunter thinks she has the brutal killer in her sights, but there's one problem. He's a Serbian war criminal who died five years earlier and lies buried in Bosnia.

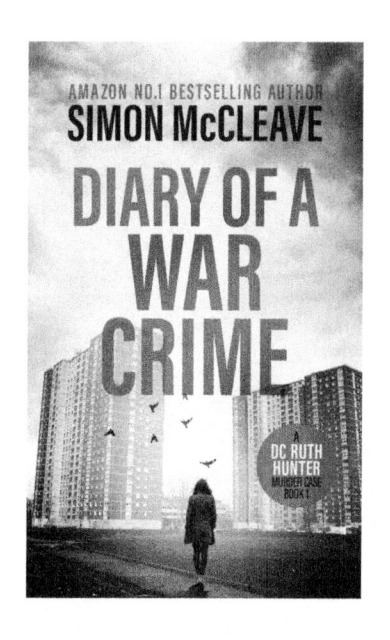

My Book
My Book

AUTHOR'S NOTE

Although this book is very much a work of fiction, it is located in Snowdonia, a spectacular area of North Wales. It is steeped in history and folklore that spans over two thousand years. I have made liberal use of artistic licence, names and places have been changed to enhance the pace and substance of the story.

Acknowledgments

I will always be indebted to the people who have made this novel possible.

My mum, Pam, and my stronger half, Nicola, whose initial reaction, ideas and notes on my work I trust implicitly. Rebecca Millar for her wonderful editing. Carole Kendal for her meticulous proofreading. My designer Stuart Bache for yet another incredible cover design. My superb agent, Millie Hoskins at United Agents, and Dave Gaughran for his invaluable support and advice.

Printed in Great Britain
by Amazon